THE CAT, THE CASH, THE LEAP & THE LIST

SUE CAMPBELL

ROOT WORD BOOKS

Text copyright © by Sue Campbell, 2019
All rights reserved. Published in the United States by Root Word Books.

Printed in the United State of America
First Printing 2018
ISBN PRINT: 978-0-578-47611-7
ISBN DIGITAL: 978-0-578-47613-1

Visit us on the Web: suecampbellbooks.com/subscribe

Root Word Books
Portland, Oregon USA

For my daughters and nephews

1

ARRIVALS

Martha knew it was a bad idea the second she'd had it. Now was not the time for such a crazy scheme. In less than an hour, a jet with her cousins on it would be touching down in Portland. She'd been waiting months for this. Well, years, actually. She'd have her cousins staying at her house for six whole weeks! Forty-two days. One thousand and eight hours.

But here she stood in some stranger's driveway, a cardboard box at her feet, and a preposterous plan formulating in her mind. A plan that could—no, *would*—get her in big trouble.

The box moved.

All the sides of the box top were folded together, creating a small rectangular opening in the middle. For the second time, Martha saw a little nose push against it.

Martha took a deep breath and marched up the junk-filled driveway. There was a red wagon with no handle, a pile of stupid Disney princess dolls, a dresser missing a drawer, and a super-ugly lamp shaped like a lion with a sign taped to it that read: *Works! $10!*

She stopped a good ten feet from the house, where a woman sat on the porch with a radio blaring. She was too tan and had a long giraffe neck.

Martha tried to swallow her anger before speaking.

"Ma'am? I'm taking that cat." She stated it boldly to try to prevent the woman from telling her to ask her parents first.

"Okay, great," the woman said. Apparently, she wasn't going to put up a fight.

"Um, does she come with anything? Like toys or a crate?"

The woman turned down the radio, just a little, before answering, "Nope. But she's free."

"And the sign says she's pregnant?"

"Yup. I can't do kittens right now. No time. I'm moving."

"But does she have any food?"

"Nope. Ran out yesterday morning," the woman shouted over a noisy radio commercial.

All the blood rushed to Martha's face. "Seriously? You haven't fed a pregnant cat since yesterday?"

The woman frowned. It seemed like she didn't like being challenged by a ten-year-old. "Are you going to take her or not, little missy?" she snarled.

Martha hesitated. She knew she had to get home right away so they could pick up the boys from the airport. She knew her parents would flip if she brought home a pregnant cat just before they had to get in the car.

The woman sat back a little and said, "Ah, I'll just take her to the shelter."

"No!" Martha almost yelled. "I'll take her." She drew a deep breath. It might not be the right time—in fact, the timing couldn't be worse—but what choice did she have?

Martha had to bite her tongue to keep from yelling at the woman about how awful it was to put a cat in a free box at a garage sale.

"Go on, then," said the woman. She turned the radio back up again, even louder than before.

Not sure what else to say, Martha turned around and walked back to the cardboard box. It had a few tiny holes in it that looked like they'd been poked with a screwdriver.

The box was too big for Martha to lug the five blocks home. She'd have to take the cat out and carry her.

The sun was burning off the clouds of the June morning, and it was getting hot. She wanted to take off her hoodie, but instead, she unzipped it most of the way, then crouched down and carefully opened the box. A large, fierce-looking gray-striped cat with yellow-green eyes gave Martha a startled look and an angry meow. Undaunted, Martha quickly scooped her up by grabbing the cat under her front legs, the equivalent of cat armpits.

The cat did not smell good. At all. But Martha had expected this.

"It's okay, little mama," Martha cooed. "I'm bringing you to live at my house, and you're going to love it. I'm really nice. I'll take good care of your kittens, too."

She stuffed the big-bellied cat down the front of her hoodie, zipped it back up, and held the cat firmly against her body. Instantly, she felt sharp claws dig into her flesh. She flinched.

"It's going to be okay, I promise," she whispered.

She stood up, and without looking back, set off for home. She heard the woman shout after her, "No returns!"

As if Martha would ever allow the cat to go back to that monster.

When she was out of sight of the house, she craned her neck to look at her watch. She didn't dare let go of her grip on the mama cat.

She was late—big-trouble late. She set off as fast as she could, which unfortunately, wasn't fast at all. By the time she passed Mrs. Foster's big green house with the wrap-around porch, she was sweating. The cat hissed and wriggled. Martha held her tighter and tried to walk faster. Her house came into sight and she exhaled in relief. Her parents were not outside. Her eyes flew to the large front windows. No expectant faces peering out at her. Good.

As she approached the side door, she took a deep breath and whispered into her chest, "Okay, shhhhhh! Be *very* quiet. You can meet everybody later." She pinned the cat to her body with only her left arm and waited a second for the cat to complain about the new arrangement. Wincing at the pawing and scratching on her belly, Martha then used her right arm to open the screen door and slip inside.

The screen door shut loudly behind her before she could catch it. Rats.

"Martha!" her mom called from upstairs. Martha grimaced.

"Yeah, Mom?" She felt the cat's body go rigid, as if she was listening, too.

"We've got to go!"

"I know, I'm sorry!"

"Meet us outside in *one* minute! We *can't* be late! We have to get all the way through security to meet them."

"Okay!"

Martha hurried to her bedroom and slammed the door. The mama cat let out an angry meow. Not daring to let her down yet, Martha pulled the quilt off her bed with one hand and threw it into the closet, which was stuffed not just with regular clothes and dress-up clothes but also yards of fabric, dozens of balls of yarn, and her entire collection of wing-tip shoes.

"I'm making you a cozy spot to rest!" whispered Martha.

The cat showed every sign of bolting, so rather than gently tucking her into the nest, Martha plopped her on top of the pile of blankets and slammed the closet door. "I'll be back soon!" she whispered at the closed door.

She looked wildly around the room for the list. She wanted to show it to Sanjay and Anand as soon as she saw them.

Her cousins lived in Minnesota and she only got to see them a few times a year. She often railed against her parents and aunt and uncle at the injustice of it all. Once, in third grade, she'd sent her aunt and uncle a certified letter begging them to move to Oregon. Cousins should get to grow up together! Especially when the oldest cousins were just six weeks apart in age and the youngest cousin had amazing chubby cheeks on a little stick body.

If they all lived in the same place, they could be together all the time. Not just to open Christmas presents and sneak extra snowflake cookies from her aunt's stash of desserts in the pantry. And not just for the five days most summers when Martha visited Minnesota and they tore around the boys' neighborhood on bikes, getting bitten up by mosquitos. (That was why Martha didn't want to move to Minnesota. She was allergic to mosquito bites. Hers always swelled into alarming blisters.)

Having the boys visit for six summer weeks was definitely a step in the right direction. And she'd made a list of all the fun they'd have so they wouldn't waste a second. She spotted her green notebook (it was on the floor mostly buried under a damp towel), grabbed it, and hurried out to the car. She'd just have to add the mama cat to the list.

Sanjay stared at the fasten-seat-belt light, willing it to turn off. The muffled, crackly voice of a flight attendant came over the loudspeaker. The only part he could make out was "Welcome to Portland, Oregon." The flight from Minneapolis took only four hours, but somehow it seemed harder than sitting still at school all day. Probably because at school there was little chance of the kid next to you having to use an airsick bag. Sanjay was just grateful that his annoying little brother managed to get all the puke in the bag and none on him.

At last, the seat belt light flicked off.

Sanjay hit Anand in the shoulder.

"Hey," Anand growled back. He still looked a little green.

"Get ready. Get your stuff," said Sanjay, then he sprang from his seat, stood on it, opened the overhead bin, and grabbed his small rolling suitcase.

"Hang on, boys," said a flight attendant. "I'll lead you two off last."

Sanjay let out a loud breath and began swatting at the name tag on his suitcase. Then he double-checked that his cycling magazine—and, more importantly, the long white envelope tucked inside of it—was safe in the front zippered compartment. His parents had put him in charge of all their spending money for the trip because he was the oldest. Anand didn't even know he had it.

Finally, the crush of people moved down the narrow aisle. Sanjay was glad to see the last of the guy with the handlebar mustache who'd been across the aisle from them and kept tapping his foot the whole flight, keeping time to whatever was playing on his gigantic headphones.

"Get your bag," Sanjay ordered. Anand scrambled to retrieve his backpack from under the seat in front of him. The hard part of the day was over. Now Anand could be his auntie and uncle's problem instead of his.

Sanjay pushed his rolling suitcase down the Jetway with one hand and pulled his little brother along with the other. The flight attendant trailed them, carrying Anand's dinosaur backpack.

As he walked out into the airport, he heard a girl's voice yell, "Sanjay!" His cousin Martha was barreling toward him. Her blond hair was much longer than the last time he'd seen her, and it was flying out behind her. In a second, she grabbed him around the chest in a bear hug and lifted him off the ground. Even though they had both just turned ten, Sanjay was a good three inches taller but so skinny Martha could easily pick him up.

"Ahhh! Put me down!" Sanjay yelled. Martha let go and

turned to Anand. He set his jaw and gave a slight shake of his head to make it known that he did not want to be picked up. Martha did it anyway.

As she plunked him down, she turned to Sanjay. "You're six minutes late," she scolded, as if he could control when an airplane landed.

Now his aunt was coming in for a hug. "Hi, Auntie Fran. Hi, Uncle Marshall." Sanjay hugged each of them. Auntie Fran squeezed too tightly. She smelled strongly of coconut oil. His uncle's beard was scratchy. He smelled like wood chips.

"Mr. and Mrs. Fitzgerald?" said the flight attendant. "The boys did very well, even though poor Anand got a little sick when we hit turbulence over Montana."

Sanjay rolled his eyes at Martha in a can-you-believe-this-kid sort of way.

While the adults were talking, Martha pulled two wing pins from the pocket of her jean shorts. "I got these from the security people. You must wear them at all times," she commanded the boys. "These show that you are in the Forty-two Days of Fun Club."

Six weeks in Portland with Martha. If he'd had the choice, he'd be going to India with his parents. But he knew he'd have fun with Martha, as long as Anand didn't ruin it by being a baby. A barfing baby.

"Okay, boys!" said Aunt Fran. "We're going to have a great time! But first, how about some food?"

"Yes, Auntie!" said Anand.

"I'm starving," said Sanjay. Their normal lunch time had long passed, and they'd eaten every granola bar, banana, and box of raisins their mom had packed. And each of them had downed three bags of pretzels the nice flight attendant had slipped them.

"We know the perfect spot," said his uncle.

"Let's go, let's go, let's go!" said Martha, leading the way.

Sanjay walked next to the bouncing Martha, leaving Anand trailing behind.

2

STICKY SITUATIONS

Wedged in the back seat between Martha and the window, Anand sighed. He was so sick of being inside moving vehicles. He felt even more trapped than he had in the airplane because Martha, with her notebook open on her lap, was hogging all the space. He hoped it didn't take long to get the restaurant. His appetite was starting to come back after being airsick.

"So, you already know there's a Forty-two Days of Fun Club," Martha was saying. "Well, there's also a Forty-two Days of Fun List!"

Anand wiggled to get comfortable, but Martha kept jabbing him in the ribs with her elbow as she went down the list.

"The zoo, the swimming pool, soccer games in the backyard, the—"

"Martha," Auntie Fran interrupted, "please save it for the restaurant. Why don't you give the boys a chance to catch their breath and look out the window?"

Martha stopped talking. Anand sent a silent thank-you to Auntie Fran. But the bouncing didn't stop.

He tried to ignore her by looking around. The sky was blue, same as back home. But unlike in Minnesota, you couldn't see for miles and miles in any direction. Portland was hilly. And busier than the town he lived in. The streets were packed with cars and bikes, and the sidewalks were full of people. It made Anand tired just looking at all the activity. He closed his eyes and wished he was in his own bedroom with a good book and a grilled cheese sandwich. And his mom and dad just in the other room.

"Look at that one!" Sanjay said as his uncle pulled up to a stop sign.

"That what?" said Martha.

They were stopped at a red light. There was a man on a shiny blue road bike right next to the car on Sanjay's side. "Whoa, check out that guy's legs!" cried Sanjay. The rider's huge thigh muscles twitched, ready to take off. Sanjay was obsessed with bikes. Anand sank into his seat.

The car moved forward again but suddenly screeched to a halt, and Anand slammed against his seat belt. His uncle yelled a bad word.

Did they just crash?

Auntie Fran turned in her seat to face the kids. "Everybody okay?" They nodded.

"Good driving, Dad," said Martha. She'd finally stopped bouncing and sat stiff. "I thought for sure we were going to hit the poor thing."

The poor what?

"I can't see!" Anand complained and craned his neck.

"That's the second time in two weeks I've almost hit a cat! They're everywhere," said Uncle Marshall.

Auntie Fran said, "I was just reading that the stray cat problem is even worse than usual this year."

"I didn't think it could get worse," said Uncle Marshall.

***

A few minutes later, Anand was crammed into a big restaurant booth with the smell of bacon, eggs, and pancakes driving him crazy with hunger. Sanjay was sitting way too close. He gave Anand's hip a little shove closer to the edge of the seat. Anand scooted away and then pointed to the flat piece of metal in the middle of the table. "What's that?" Anand asked.

"It's a griddle, stupid," said Sanjay.

"Hey, be nice to your little brother," Martha said sharply. She turned to Anand. "You make your own pancakes right at the table. See?" She pointed across the aisle where some kids were flipping humongous pancakes with a plastic spatula. "Everybody should just order batter so we can make the pancakes ourselves and get out of here fast."

"What's your hurry, Martha?" asked Uncle Marshall.

"Oh, I'm just excited to get this visit started!" Martha said. "But be careful, once they turn on the griddle, it gets hot really fast."

"Yes, it does!" said the waiter, who'd just walked up. "What can I get for you folks today?"

As Anand stared at the tattooed forearms of the waiter, Martha ordered batter and toppings for the whole table.

He especially liked the glistening green mermaid whose tail seemed to flick as the waiter fiddled with the knobs on the griddle. Anand wanted a tattoo someday, a big T. rex, but he wasn't sure where he wanted it.

"Now, while we wait, you can read this," said Martha, pushing her notebook in front of the boys. Anand reached for it, but Sanjay snatched it and pulled it closer to him.

"The Forty-Two Days of Fun List," Sanjay read aloud.

Martha bounced on the vinyl seat.

"Oh wow, it's illustrated even," Sanjay said, turning pages too fast for Anand to read them. "Um, there are a hundred and twelve things on this list, Martha. We're only here for forty-two days."

"I know. We'll have to do two to three things per day. We've already done one just by being here," Martha said.

She took the notebook back and used the pen tucked behind her ear to scratch off item number twenty-one: trip to Flappy Jacks.

The waiter came back with their pancake stuff. There were two squeeze bottles of batter. Best of all, there were about a dozen little metal cups full of toppings: blueberries, bananas, hazelnuts, even chocolate chips. Sanjay swiped the chocolate chip cup before Anand could.

Anand picked up a batter bottle and squeezed out a lumpy stegosaurus. Martha made a butterfly and a dog. Sanjay made a sailboat and a bike. Uncle Marshall grabbed a batter bottle and squeezed out a cat. When the edges of his stegosaurus were bubbly, Anand flipped it over. It was perfectly golden brown.

"You guys seem a little tired after your flight," said Aunt Fran. "Just imagine how tired your parents will be, going from Minnesota to India. They're still in the air right now."

"It's twenty hours on an airplane!" Anand said. The thought was horrible. Uncle Marshall whistled in a that-is-impressive sort of way.

They chatted about the excitement of a trip to India, even if the reason for the trip was a sad one. The boys' great-grandfather, their dad's grandpa, was very old and sick.

"My dad says he's glad that he'll get to see him one last time," said Sanjay. "My mom is sad that she has to be without us for over a month. And my dad is, too, of course."

"I know that was a tough choice for them to make," said Uncle Marshall.

Anand looked at his brother. Sanjay had thrown a fit when their parents told them they wouldn't be going along on this trip. Now, Sanjay said, "Yeah. We'll get to go next year maybe. Or the year after. They said."

Martha shoved half a pancake in her mouth and said, "I can't believe we get to spend forty-two days together!"

Anand looked down at his plate. It seemed like forever to be away from his mom and dad.

"Martha! Slow down," Auntie Fran said. "You're going to choke."

Martha's eyes got big and her chewing slowed down.

Auntie Fran turned to Anand. "How are you feeling, Anand? Do you still feel sick, or were you just airsick from the plane?"

Sanjay said, "It's just because of the plane. He pukes on

long car trips sometimes, too. And boat rides. And escalators."

Anand scowled at him. It was so embarrassing. His mom kept saying he'd outgrow it.

"Are you feeling better after eating?" asked Martha, who had finally managed to swallow. "Ready to hear about the rest of the fun I have planned?"

Anand nodded.

Martha opened her mouth to speak but her mom cut her off, "First I want to ask the boys, is there anything that *you* really want to do while you're here? Martha doesn't get to make *all* the decisions."

Anand said, "I want to see—"

"The ocean!" Sanjay said.

It was one thing they agreed on. And it was the thing their mom had kept reminding them about to get them excited. They'd get to spend time at the ocean.

The tattooed waiter came back and leaned over Anand to clear their plates.

"Out of the way," Sanjay scolded and gave him another hip check. This time, he did it so hard it pushed Anand out of the booth and onto the floor. Anand wailed. He felt his uncle scoop him up off the floor. Something was dripping off him. Blood? He looked down. No, milk and maple syrup.

"Aw, man," Sanjay sighed and slid down lower in the booth to hide.

"You pushed me!" Anand yelled at him and cradled his arm to his chest.

"I was just trying to keep you out of the waiter's way,"

Sanjay shot back. "I didn't think you'd fall. Any other kid would have caught himself."

"Are you hurt?" Martha began to inspect him, making sure he could move his arms. "Did you break anything?" Anand was too mad to feel any pain. He glared at her without answering.

"Give him a little space, Martha," said Uncle Marshall.

Aunt Fran inspected him. "I don't think there's any permanent damage. Anything still hurt, buddy?"

Anand shook his head fiercely. Why was everyone treating him like a baby? He was eight years old!

"We have to get him home. Right now," said Martha to her mom.

Anand flinched a little at the word "home."

3

THE CLOSET DOOR OPENS

Martha's right leg jittered up and down as she sat in the back seat chewing her hair. This was terrible. She hadn't chewed her own hair since second grade when they'd had that terrifying German lady as a substitute teacher for over a month. Sanjay grabbed her knee and pressed on it.

"Oh, sorry," she said. But she started right back up again. They had been gone too long! Mama Cat would be freaking out. Martha hadn't even had time to leave her any food or water.

The instant the car stopped in the driveway, Martha shouted, "Race you to the backyard!" They sprang from their seats and bolted up the driveway. She flung open the gate to the backyard and cried, "Garden post is the finish line!" She was slightly ahead, since she had the home-field advantage. Charlie, her big yellow Labrador, bounded up into second place, tail wagging excitedly. She grabbed the fence post at the edge of the garden and swung herself around it in a little victory dance. Sanjay was third, with Anand in last place and shirtless. Martha had told him to take his shirt off in the car because it was covered in milk and syrup. She didn't want him bothering to change once they got home. Now the boys were just where she wanted them.

"You guys explore the backyard. I've gotta go to the bathroom!"

She sprinted back to the house and paused at the door to collect herself. As casually as she could manage, she walked into the kitchen. Her parents were standing at the dining room table sorting through a stack of mail.

Martha tucked herself around the corner out of view of the table. She pulled a bowl down. She got a glass, filled it with water, and walked to her room.

She heard her dad ask, "Where are the boys, Martha?"

"Outside!" she yelled without turning around.

Back in her room, she poured the water into the bowl and opened the closet door a small crack. The cat pushed her head against the door, trying to get out.

Martha quickly closed the door again. She had to think. Was it safe to let the cat out of the closet and into the room? She had to risk it. She couldn't let her go without water any longer.

Martha set the bowl down just outside the sweep of the door and then opened the door wide and stepped back across the room.

The cat came flying out of the closet and jumped on Martha's bed, looking around wildly for an exit. She tore across the room, and when she couldn't find a way out, bolted under the bed.

Martha pushed the bowl in after her, gave a deep sigh, and slipped out of the room.

She found the boys in the middle of the long, narrow backyard. Sanjay was stretched out in the hammock with Anand squatting on the ground next to him, petting Charlie, apparently waiting for his turn to swing. Of course, they wouldn't sit in it together. Martha thought she might need to have a talk with Sanjay about being nicer to Anand.

"So, what do we do first?" Sanjay asked.

"Well," said Martha slowly. She was about to tell them about the cat but stopped herself. "You have to get unpacked, of course. But first, let's meet the chickens, and I'll show you where we're going to build the fort tomorrow. We need a base of operations."

Martha led them back through the vegetable garden to the chicken yard. She plucked a handful of dandelion greens and poked them through the wire fence. Five fat hens came running from the underbrush and started pulling the greens away from them.

Martha rattled off the names of the hens while pointing out each one: "Ginger, Ricki, Colonel Sanders, Buttercup, and the big black one is Andre. She's a Jersey Giant."

"Whoa!" said Sanjay. "That chicken is *huge*. She's as big as my neighbor's dog!"

"She's heavy, too," said Martha nonchalantly. "But she's scared of everything. And she eats the most and doesn't lay eggs anymore, but we love her anyway."

"What's the cat's name?" Anand asked, pointing to a

large black cat that was hunched in the back corner of the chicken yard.

Martha gulped. "Don't know. It's not ours. There are a bunch of cats that run around the neighborhood," she said. "They're feral—you know, wild. Like the one my dad almost hit." She had to get the conversation away from cats! "Come on," she said, "let's collect some eggs."

Martha led the way inside the coop.

The first thing she saw was a big orange cat curled up in one of the nesting boxes. "Shoo! Shoo!" she said, waving her arms wildly. It was like cats were haunting her!

The cat scrambled and dashed out the door.

Each nest box was filled with straw, and several had eggs in them.

Martha pulled up the bottom edges of her T-shirt to make an egg basket. "Load me up," she said.

Sanjay loaded the eggs into her shirt until it nearly overflowed and then handed the last two to Anand—a brown one and a blue one.

"Colonel Sanders lays the blue ones," Martha said just as Sanjay swung the door of the coop open and it came rushing toward Anand. He reached out his hands to stop it, smashing the eggs he was holding.

Martha doubled over in laughter and almost dropped all the eggs cradled in her shirt. Sanjay was laughing and shaking his head. Anand's cheeks got red.

"It's okay. Come on," Martha said, leading them back to the house.

Charlie intercepted them, nosing at Anand's eggy hands.

"It tickles!" Anand squealed.

Martha saw an opportunity.

"Listen," Martha leaned in and lowered her voice. "We'll go inside and get you washed up, but then there's something important we need to do right away, and it means you have to *swear* to keep a secret."

Anand was wide-eyed.

"Uh oh," said Sanjay.

A few minutes later, the boys had been briefed, and Martha gave Anand a gentle nudge through the door. "Go show them your eggy hands," she hissed at him. "We need a diversion! Go, go!"

Martha counted to sixty and then she and Sanjay tiptoed into the kitchen pantry. Martha shoved things aside until she found what she was looking for: a can of tuna. She grabbed it and turned around, nodding to Sanjay. They could hear Anand talking to her mom and dad in the living room. They tiptoed across the kitchen, and Sanjay cracked open Martha's bedroom door. He whispered, "I think she's still under the bed."

As the last word was coming out of his mouth, the cat streaked by through the slightly open door and bolted down the hallway toward the living room.

Martha and Sanjay dashed after her. Anand yelled in surprise. Soon Martha's parents joined in the yelling. "What on earth is going on? Martha, where did the cat come from?" The cat tore around the room then scurried under the couch.

Martha froze, staring at her parents. They stared back

at her. Finally, Martha's dad broke the silence. "Martha, *explain.*"

"I, um..." Martha struggled to come up with a story that would keep her out of trouble. She decided there probably wasn't one.

"I got her at a garage sale this morning. They had her in a free box! They were going to give her to just anybody! I had to rescue her!"

Her parents stared at her. Finally, her mom said, "Oh, Martha," and shook her head.

"Why didn't you ask?" said her dad.

"There wasn't time!" Her heart was pounding and tears were ready to burst from her eyes. "We were about to go get the boys, and I didn't want to get in a fight right before we went. And I knew you'd say no. I had to save her!" And then all the tears came out at once.

"Oh, Martha," her mother said again.

"Come on, Martha, help me get her out from under the couch. We have to take her back."

"No!" Martha sobbed hard. "Dad! We can't bring her back! The woman was horrible! What kind of person would give away a pregnant cat?!"

"She's pregnant?" yelled her mother.

Her father stood with his feet firmly planted on the rug, his arms rigid and hovering about six inches from his sides. He looked like he was preparing to raise his hands and shoot lightning out of this fingertips. He took a breath and said, "Let me get this straight. You adopted a pregnant cat that you found in a free box just five minutes before going to pick up your cousins and without asking us first? Do I have that right?"

"Yes," said Martha in a small voice.

"Go to your room."

"But—" said Martha, looking toward the couch with the angry cat under it.

"Leave the cat."

Martha scooted down the hall as fast as she could. Out of the corner of her eye, she saw her mom plop down on the couch and heard her give an exasperated groan. Mama Cat wailed.

Martha closed the door of her room and slid down the wall, sobbing. She would lose Mama Cat. Her parents would take her back to that awful woman, or worse, a shelter. Martha wouldn't get to raise the kittens. She wouldn't even ever get to see them.

She took a deep breath. She had to show she could be responsible, starting with cleaning up the closet.

She looked in the closet. It was a horrible sight. And smell. The cat had pulled her clothes down from the hangers and strewn them everywhere. The blankets she'd put in for a cat bed were soaking wet. And not with water. Her nose wrinkled at the smell of cat pee. Pregnant cat pee.

"Foul," she muttered, picking up the blankets and clothes, careful to touch only dry areas.

She quietly opened the door and took all the blankets down to the laundry room. Martha had been doing her own laundry since the age of seven. She knew a mess like this called for plenty of soap, an extra rinse cycle, and a glug of the special cleaner they saved for when Charlie puked on something.

There was no actual ceiling in the unfinished basement, only the wood that created the floor of the room above. That meant it was a good place to listen in on adult conversations happening upstairs. But she could only hear the murmurs of her parents' voices. They were being quiet on purpose.

Martha scampered up onto a shelf and stood so her ear was just a few feet from the ceiling. She could only pick out a few words. The loudest of them was "consequences."

It wasn't sounding good.

The talking stopped and footsteps started. Uh-oh.

"Martha!"

"Coming!" she yelled.

4

SIX RAFTERS BACK

Sanjay stood in the living room, shifting uncomfortably from foot to foot. His auntie had just called for Martha, and he followed the sound of her thumping up from the basement. A second later she came in panting.

"I sent you to your room, Martha. Why were you in the basement?" Uncle Marshall asked her.

"Sorry," she said. "The mama cat had a little, um, accident in my closet, so I started a load of laundry."

"Your closet?" her mom asked.

"That's where I put her while we went to the airport."

Sanjay shook his head. Unbelievable.

Auntie Fran took a deep breath. "Okay, Martha, here's the deal. And it's non-negotiable, so listen carefully. Boys, there's a part for you in this, too. And you don't have to agree to these terms if you don't want to. First off, Martha, you owe the boys an apology."

Sanjay started to say, "No, she—" but Martha interrupted.

"Yes, I do. I'm so sorry! You guys haven't even been here two hours, and I've got you in the middle of a big family fight. Maybe the biggest one ever."

Sanjay heard his uncle mutter something about wishing for all future ones to be smaller.

"Okay, now the terms," his aunt continued. "We are *not* adopting this cat."

"But—" Martha started, but Auntie Fran put up her palm.

"Don't even, Martha. We don't know anything about this cat. She could have a disease for all we know. We're going to take her to the vet and get her checked out, and then if the vet says she's in good health, we can *foster* her. We are *not* her forever home. *You* will find her a forever family."

Martha looked miserable, and he could see why.

"Also, all expenses for this will come from *your* personal savings," Auntie Fran went on. Martha kept on nodding.

"You will do *all* the work, including feedings, litter box cleaning, and whatever else is needed. The boys can help, *if* they choose. But you are not to *direct* them to help."

"We'll help!" chirped Anand. Sanjay gave him the side-eye.

"You must also find foster or forever homes for *all* the kittens she ends up having."

Sanjay watched Martha's jaw tighten. She obviously wanted to object but thought better of it.

"You are also grounded for *one month,* starting the instant the boys get on the plane to go back to Minnesota."

A month! That beat Sanjay's record by two weeks.

"Boys, you need to unpack and get to bed. You've had a long day," said Auntie Fran. "Martha, you're coming with me to get cat supplies. Go get your money."

Sanjay led Anand up the creaky stairs to the guest room. It was noticeably hotter up here. Sanjay took a deep breath before unzipping his backpack. His parents were a zillion miles away, his cousin moved at a zillion miles an hour. It all made him feel like that time he got the wind knocked out of him during a kickball game.

"The top bunk is mine. Obviously," he warned Anand.

Anand climbed into the bottom bunk, which had curtains all around it. "Fine with me," he said and quickly drew them closed.

Sanjay opened the top drawer of the small dresser he'd be sharing with Anand for the next forty-two days. He turned his backpack upside down and shook his clothes into the drawer. They didn't take up much room, being mostly shorts, T-shirts, and swim trunks.

A family picture fluttered out of the bag and landed on the top of the pile. It had been taken at the Holi festival at the start of spring. Right before the photo was snapped, they'd been throwing handfuls of Holi powder at each other. All their faces were coated in splotches of rainbow colors, and his mom—looking a lot like Auntie Fran, funny that he'd never noticed that before—was so happy and smiley.

He put the picture in his pocket and reached his hand into the front pouch of his suitcase to make sure his bike magazines were still there but didn't take them out yet. He had to get Anand out of the room first. His unpacking done, he crawled into the top bunk. There was a chocolate-covered mint on his pillow. *Nice touch, Martha.* He popped it into his mouth and sat crossed-legged, slowly sucking the chocolate coating off the mint.

Sanjay was severely annoyed about sharing a room with his brother—back home they each had their own bedroom. But at least there was someone he could talk to about the huge family fight they were now in the middle of.

"I can't believe they're letting her foster that cat. We could never get away with the stuff she does," said Sanjay.

Anand stuck his head out from behind the curtains. "They were pretty mad though," he said.

"Yeah. But they're okay. They're not mad at us."

"Do you think we'll be too busy with the cats to do any Forty-two Days of Fun stuff?" Anand asked.

"No, Martha will still want to do *all* of that, too. Just watch. She won't give up a thing."

"She's kinda stubborn, huh?"

"Yes. But you don't have to do everything she says. Pick your battles, like Mom says." Sanjay reached in his pocket and felt the sharp edge of the photograph.

"Well, I don't mind helping with the cat. I've never seen kittens just born."

"Me neither," said Sanjay. He took the picture out and

looked at it one more time before tucking it under his pillow. He grabbed the bunk-bed railing and leaned out until he was looming over the bottom bunk. "I know we're sharing a room," he said in a warning tone. "But you better stay off my top bunk and out of my drawers."

Anand's face changed into an angry pucker. "*You* stay out of *mine*. And don't be a slob!" Anand snatched the curtains closed.

"Go get ready for bed," said Sanjay. "You're cranky and need to sleep."

"Don't tell me what to do," huffed Anand. But he grabbed his toothbrush and headed downstairs.

Sanjay waited until he was at the bottom of the steps before getting down from the bunk and opening the drawer that was full of Anand's tidy piles of stuff. The headlamp was right on top of the pile, as he knew it would be. It was Anand's most prized possession. He didn't have much time. He put the headlamp on, then pulled the long envelope out of his stack of magazines. He quickly fanned out the fat wad of five- and ten-dollar bills, all three hundred dollars of it.

And Sanjay wasn't going to spend a dime of it. He was going to save it all for a new bike. He was getting too big for his old one, and he needed something more pro. He tucked the envelope into the waistband of his shorts and covered it with his T-shirt.

In his stocking feet, he soundlessly walked across the hall into his aunt's dark office. The beam of the headlamp fell on piles of unfinished knitting and a big bookcase stuffed with yarn instead of books. The desk in the corner was piled with still more knitting and stacks of papers.

There was a small half door in the wall that opened onto a crawl space created by the steeply angled roof. Sanjay knew about it from the last time he'd visited and played hide-and-seek with Martha. He'd spent forever searching for her. She had been deep inside, finally giving herself away by sneezing from her dusty hiding place.

Sanjay pushed aside a big cardboard box blocking the doorway. Whatever was inside rattled loudly. He froze for second to make sure no one heard. Then he bent over and walked about halfway in. The beam from the headlamp created a slice of orange light and revealed thick dust in the air. Just seeing the dust made Sanjay want to sneeze. The angled walls were covered with fiberglass insulation, and nails stuck out of the ceiling from the roof shingles above.

Sanjay heard the faint whoosh of a toilet flushing and then a faucet running. Anand would be back soon. He took out the envelope and pushed it deeply between a board and the insulation, careful not to touch the fiber-glass. He remembered his dad's warning about itchy fiber-glass from when he had insulated their attic. Sanjay counted the rafters back to the door so he could remember the spot where the envelope was hidden. Six rafters back.

He popped out of the crawl space and walked quickly out of the room. As he came onto the landing, Anand appeared at the bottom of the stairs.

"Hey!" said Anand. "That's *my* headlamp!" and ran up the steps with his hand outstretched.

"Relax, I was only playing with it."

"I told you to stay out of my stuff! You'll run out the batteries. Give it back! Now!"

Sanjay pulled it off and handed it back without a fight. Anand put it on, then jumped onto the bottom bunk and stuck out his bottom lip in a pout before snatching the curtains closed.

Sanjay climbed into the top bunk, bringing a recent issue of *Adventure Cycling* up with him. When he switched on the reading lamp, he noticed a glint of fiberglass. *Aw, man*, he thought. He held his hands over the side of the bed and brushed them against each other, not wanting to get any scratchy fiberglass in his sheets. Already his right hand itched from the stuff.

He lay staring at the ceiling and listening to his brother thrashing around below him. Sanjay had dreaded this first night away from home. He was sure Anand would freak out. But he didn't hear any sniffling or whimpering. Maybe he was just too mad to cry.

The rustling from the bunk below stopped, and soon after, Sanjay heard deep, steady breathing. He could still see a glow from the headlamp, so he climbed down and switched it off.

He heard someone coming up the stairs. Auntie Fran poked her head in.

"Is he asleep?" she whispered and pointed to the closed curtains.

Sanjay nodded. She walked over to him.

"Is there anything you need?"

He shook his head. She put a hand on either side of his face and tilted his head down so she could kiss the top of it.

"Goodnight. I told Martha to go to bed, too, so she won't be back up here tonight," she said and tiptoed out.

Forty-one days to go. As exciting as it was to be with Martha, he would have loved to be in India instead. He wanted to see it all for himself, this place his father had grown up in. And being away from his parents—when he knew they were half a world away—bothered him. Though he'd never admit it to Martha, or Anand. He worried about plane crashes or his mom getting hit by motorcycles that his dad said were so common in India. It hadn't helped that shortly before they left he had caught his mom reading something called *How to Drive in India Without Dying.*

Sanjay sighed and settled into his bunk, looking at bikes and scratching his right hand until he finally fell asleep.

5

THE FORT

Martha awoke the next morning to a quiet house. Her first thought was of Mama Cat. She threw off her covers, tiptoed over to the closet, and peered in. The gray tabby was sleeping peacefully on her new cat bed, her big belly hanging over the edge.

"Oh good," Martha whispered. "You're sleeping in. You need your rest."

She crept out of her room and went to the kitchen. While Martha was opening a can of cat food, Charlie came in from the living room, nails clicking across the wood floors. He snuffled her good morning.

"Hey, buddy. I know you're good with cats, but I'm not so sure this cat is good with dogs. You better stay out of my room, okay?" She gave him her finger to lick a tiny morsel of sticky cat food.

Back in her bedroom, she set the food bowl down next to Mama Cat, who was now awake and eyeing Martha warily. "I brought you breakfast." She was keeping her tone light and soft. "You can just stay where you are. I've got loads to do today, but I'll come and check on you a bunch. I'm going to go wake up the boys."

She padded back to the kitchen got out a pan and a baking sheet, slamming them down on top of the stove, pretty much directly below where the boys were nestled in their bunks. Her mom came in and put a finger to her lips.

A half hour later, the boys came slogging sleepily down the steps. Martha gave a little squeal of delight and swept a welcoming arm toward the table she'd set just as the oven timer went off. She scurried to retrieve her biscuits from the oven.

"Good timing, boys" said Mom. "I was about to let Martha up to wake you."

"She *did* wake us," said Sanjay grumpily.

"It's eight thirty your time," Martha chided.

Anand took a bite of breakfast. "These are the best eggs I've ever had."

"Those are the eggs you guys collected. Well, what's left of them," Martha's mom said, giving Anand a grin. "Hey, I was thinking. I need to add something to your Forty-Two Days of Fun List."

Martha raised an eyebrow. "The list is already pretty full, Mom."

Her mom ignored her and turned to the boys.

"I think Friday nights should be the boys' pick. We can do something that you guys would normally do at home. I could even get some Indian food recipes from your mom and try those out."

"Yes!" said Sanjay.

"I'll help cook, but I don't want to eat it," said Anand.

"What?" said Martha. "That doesn't make any sense."

"He doesn't like Indian food," said Sanjay. "But I do! He can have a grilled cheese or something."

"Fine with me," said Anand.

"Great. And think up some other stuff you'd like to do. Maybe watch your favorite movie?" said her mom. "Martha, can you add this to your—"

"Already doing it," Martha cut her off, her nose in her notebook.

After breakfast, Martha stood with her dad and the boys, surveying the garden. "This will be our outdoor base of operations," she said.

The site she'd picked for the fort was hemmed in by a thick hedge on one side, the wall of the chicken coop on another, and a fence along the back. It was nice and private, but it was filled with vines and prickers and the earthy smell of chicken poop.

She had all the building materials ready. There were pruning shears and a hedge trimmer, work gloves for everyone, wooden pallets, a pile of tarps, three hammers, a box of nails, some wood screws, a power drill, and a stack of used lumber.

"Do you know how to use all this stuff?" Sanjay asked.

"Of course! This guy taught me," said Martha, jabbing a thumb behind her toward her dad. "I'll show you what you need to know. But first we have to clear the vines." She passed an electric hedge trimmer to her dad and pruning shears to Sanjay.

"Anand, run and get the wheelbarrow. It's in the chicken yard by the pear tree," said Martha. Her dad cleared his throat and exchanged a look with her mom, who was lying in the hammock knitting.

He leaned in and whispered in her ear, "Listen, kiddo, your cousins are on *vacation*. Make it fun and be nice or you'll be facing a mutiny."

Martha sighed.

"Hey, Anand," she tried again. "Can you *please* grab that super-fun wheelbarrow over there? And watch out for chicken and cat poop." Anand ran to get it.

Martha's dad and Sanjay cut back the vines. Martha loaded the trimmings into the wheelbarrow, and Anand struggled to push the loads to the bin where they kept yard waste. After a solid half hour of work, they were all sweating. Martha's mom brought out ice waters, and Martha drank hers down in a few gulps, the cold water making her gasp when she was done.

"I'm covered in scratches from these vines!" said Sanjay, staring at his outstretched arms, which now had angry red marks above his gloves.

"I guess I should have told you to wear long sleeves," said Martha.

"Ya think?" Sanjay said sarcastically.

Martha shrugged. "Don't worry, we're done brush clearing. Now we're ready for building!" She opened her notebook to show her work crew a rough blueprint of how the fort should be built. Martha and Sanjay dragged the pallets, which would form three sides of the structure, into the new clearing.

"The door needs to face away from the house and toward the hedge," said Martha, smiling at her dad. "For privacy from grown-ups."

They nailed two pallets together for the back wall, then one on each side. Martha had her dad reinforce the corners with wood screws, and she and Sanjay did most of the hammering. Anand's nail-pounding skills were terrible, so she said, "Hey, Anand, why don't you make us a nice wooden box for supplies?" She gave him some scrap wood and showed him how to build a simple box, which they didn't really need but would keep him out of the way while they finished construction.

Once the three walls were up, they spread a canvas tarp over the top for the roof. They strung another canvas tarp across the opening to serve as a door. Her dad helped them fashion a rope so they could tie the tarp back if they wanted extra air or light.

Martha stood back to inspect their work. It was pretty basic, and she wished it was a tree house, but it would do. There was only one decent tree in the whole yard, the pear tree, and it didn't have the right kind of branches for a tree-house. When Martha was younger she was forever spitting her apple seeds in the yard, but she finally realized by the time it was big enough, she'd be a grown-up and out of the house. She picked up her notebook from the ground and scratched "fort building" off the Forty-Two Days of Fun List. Nothing felt better than checking something off a list.

"There," she said with a firm nod.

"Oh, good. I'm *so* glad we're keeping the list updated," Sanjay mocked.

Martha decided to ignore his bad mood. "That was fun," she said. "And now, furnishings. Come on." They went back to the house and collected a step stool and a big stack of books from Martha's bedroom and said hi to Mama Cat. She hissed at them.

"Sanjay, can you go downstairs and grab the red cooler?"

"What for?"

"For snacks!" she said. "We never have to go hungry!"

"Good idea," said Sanjay, and he went downstairs.

"Anand, you get the door for me, and I'll carry all this stuff."

They made one more trip for blankets and pillows and scattered them on the floor of the fort. Sanjay and Anand looked ready to throw themselves down when Martha cried, "Wait! Before we use this fort, I must cast a protective spell on it." She searched her brain for an appropriate spell. Since she couldn't come up with anything that rhymed and was sufficiently reverent, she settled for muttering under her breath, *"Stay out, stay out, stay out."* She scooped up handfuls of dirt and sprinkled them all around the outside. Then she stood at the entrance, imagining an invisible force field surrounding the fort, and humming in what she hoped was a hypnotic way. *That should do it*, she thought. She motioned the boys inside with a sweep of her arm and a solemn nod.

"What are we protecting the fort from, exactly?" asked Sanjay.

"Oh, you know, evil spirits, coyotes, cat poop, that sort

of thing."

"Uh-huh," said Sanjay.

They plopped down onto the soft pillows. The sunlight filtering through the tarp did make the inside of the fort seem somehow enchanted, which pleased Martha.

"It's a good fort," said Anand.

"Yes. Well done, you two," said Martha. "Settle in. I'll be right back." She went out to the garden and scavenged the strawberry bed for the reddest, ripest berries. She popped one in her mouth. Sweetness exploded on her tongue. She ducked back in the fort and shared her harvest.

"Yum!" Anand said.

From far off, she heard her mom calling: "Martha! Sanjay! Anand! Lunch! Come and get it!"

They found her in the kitchen with two steaming pizza boxes.

"Pizza!" Martha squealed. "It's the perfect food!"

"Before you eat, why don't you go check on Mama Cat and make sure she has everything she needs," said her mom.

"Then can we take the pizza out to the fort to eat?"

"Of course."

Martha dashed across the hall to her bedroom with the boys behind her. She stopped short.

"Uh-oh. The door's open."

"Did you leave it open when you got the furniture for the fort?" asked Sanjay.

Martha got a bad feeling in the very bottom of her stomach.

"Maybe." She tiptoed into the room. "Mama Cat?" she

called in a whisper, so as not to startle her.

"Maybe she's asleep," whispered Martha.

"Uh, maybe?" said Sanjay skeptically.

They peered into the partly open closet.

No rustling. No glimpse of stripy gray fur.

"Mama Cat?" Martha whispered again, not wanting to believe her eyes and ears.

She dropped to her knees and turned over the cat bed and blankets.

Nothing. Just the lingering smell of a cat pee.

"Mom!" Martha screamed. "Mom, Mom, Mom!"

Her mother came rushing into the room.

"She's gone! The door was open!" Martha cried. "She's gone!" Tears were already spurting from her eyes.

"Hang on, Martha," said her mother in her soothing tone. "She's probably in the house somewhere. There's no need to panic."

They all spread out across the house. Martha continued crying as she searched every dark corner and under every piece of furniture. The boys looked in the basement, and when they didn't find her, Martha double-checked. Her mom searched upstairs with no luck. Martha searched again. With each potential hiding place that was discovered empty, Martha's panic grew.

She stood in the doorframe to the closet in her parents' room. Her eyes felt hot and puffy from crying. It was time to face reality. In all the opening and closing of doors and the chaos of fort building, Mama Cat had escaped from the house.

She planted both her feet and yelled, "Family meeting! Everybody to the living room!"

6

THE SEARCH

Even though Martha had called the meeting, it took a minute before she could actually speak. She stood rooted in the center living room rug, staring out at her mom, dad, and cousins, taking very deep breaths and trying to hold in her crying.

"I think," she finally began between gasps, "she got away. She got outside."

Her dad came up and put his arms around her. She hugged him, then broke away.

"We've gotta go look outside."

"I'm sorry!" she burst out. "Sanjay, Anand, this wasn't how the trip was supposed to go! This is *not* fun."

"It's okay, Martha!" said Sanjay, while Anand nodded furiously. "We'll find her and get her back."

"Then we'll have fun," said Anand.

Martha took another very deep breath to calm herself. "Okay. We'll go look all over the neighborhood, and if we can't find her, we'll have to make signs and post them and recruit some neighbors to help search."

"Sounds like a plan," said her dad.

"Let's go," said Sanjay.

"Anand, you don't know the neighborhood yet, so stay with me," said Martha, returning to her calmer self. "Sanjay, you check all the yards that touch ours. Mom and Dad, you go farther out."

Martha sprinted to the backyard, Anand straggling behind. She stopped at the very back of the yard, past the garden and behind the chicken coop.

"We'll start here and work our way back toward the house." Martha was speaking low, hoping not to spook Mama Cat. "Don't yell for her or anything. She didn't really know us very well yet and probably wants to hide from us. Check all the underneath spaces you see, the bushes, those kinds of places."

Martha was calmer and focused now. Taking action always helped her. There was a fence right behind the chicken coop, dividing her yard from the neighbors to the north. The narrow space between the fence and the chicken coop was filled with prickly, overgrown blackberry bushes and Martha couldn't squeeze into it. She groaned and fell to her knees, then leaned down as close to cat level as she could and pressed her face to the fence. She squinted to see better. But there was no glimpse of fur, no glowing cat eyes.

On the other side of the coop, there were gaps in the wooden siding that let neighborhood cats get underneath it.

She stuck her eye to one of the holes. It was so dark

under there that she couldn't have seen the cat if she was just a foot away, so she put her ear to the hole instead. She listened for any rustling or meowing. But there was no noise from under the coop, just the sounds of her own chickens giving the occasional soft cluck as they scratched around for worms under the pear tree. Anand came up beside her.

"Is she under there?" he whispered.

"I don't hear anything."

"My teacher said cats liked to find secret places to have kittens. She thought she lost her cat once, but she was just hiding."

Fresh panic rose in her as she realized this must be the case.

"Oh no! That's it! She escaped because it's time to have her kittens! What if the kittens die because Mama Cat is all alone? We've got to keep searching."

They combed through the rest of the backyard and then the front, though there weren't many good hiding places up there. Tears welled up in Martha's eyes again and she stuck two fingers in her mouth and gave her loudest whistle. Within a moment, Sanjay and her parents appeared. She looked hopefully at the arms of each, but none of them were cradling a cat.

"Okay, everybody report! Where did you check?" As each person reported on where they'd searched. Martha whipped out her notebook and quickly sketched out a map of the neighborhood map, putting an X on the areas they'd checked.

"Mom, we need to go to the art supply store." She turned to Sanjay and Anand. "We've got to make posters.

Not cheesy ones you can't read from a moving car. Good ones. I'll go get my money."

"Now?" asked her mom. "We need to go this second?"

"Yes!"

"Martha, I know you're worried, and I'm trying to be understanding here, but let's give ourselves a chance to take a breath. I want all three of you to go eat some pizza, and then we'll go to the store."

Martha was about to protest when she caught the warning look on her dad's face.

"Fine," she sighed.

The pizza was cold by the time they got back to the house.

"Eat fast," she instructed.

"I don't think I could eat slow at this point. I'm starving," said Sanjay.

Martha began to feel better as she ate. Crying was exhausting! And she needed all the strength and energy she could get if she was going to find Mama Cat.

"Okay," she said when they'd each gobbled down a couple of slices. "Anand, go take a bathroom break so we can tell Mom we did that already and get going!"

"Do you think we'll actually find her?" Sanjay asked.

"Of course," said Martha. "These posters are going to be so amazing, someone will see her and call us."

"Do you have any pictures of her? For the signs?"

Martha frowned. "No."

"Well, then I hope you're good at drawing pregnant cats," said Sanjay dryly.

"As a matter of fact," Martha replied, "I am."

7

POSTERS AND A TARZAN ROPE

Anand sat very still at the dining room table and narrowed his eyes, as if that would somehow help him hear his mom's voice better. He pictured the globe in his classroom and imagined his mom as a tiny dot on the other side of the world from him. That's how far away she sounded. Her voice cut in and out. She warned him that they might not be able to talk for long before the connection was lost.

She said they'd made it to Dad's hometown of Pilani and visited a temple there.

Saraswati Temple, it was called. To Anand, it sounded like the name of a pretty girl.

When she asked him how he was, he wanted to cry.

But he couldn't, not with his aunt and uncle right there. He tightened up the muscles in his face and tried to think of something happy to say, but all that came out was "Martha got a pregnant cat from a garage sale, but she ran away! We have to find her!"

Instead of the excited reaction he expected, the phone was quiet.

Anand held out the phone. "Auntie Fran, she had to hang up."

"I'm sure it was a bad connection. We can try again later," said Auntie Fran.

"Right now we're going to put up signs around the neighborhood," said Martha. "And then we're going swimming!"

"We are?" asked Anand, confused. He was trying to shake off the sadness of the call. "But shouldn't we find your cat first?"

"We've got a Forty-two Day of Fun List to get through. We'll hang up the signs, then go swimming, and by the time we get home, someone will have called about the cat and we can go pick her up," said Martha, sounding so sure of herself that Anand looked at Sanjay for confirmation. Sanjay shrugged.

Out at the backyard shed, Martha put the cat posters in her bike basket and strapped them down. Anand didn't know exactly how many cat posters there were, but it was a thick stack, each one with a hand-drawn cartoon cat with a big pregnant belly. Anand's job had been to color in the stripes. Martha and Sanjay had written most of the message inside the belly of the cat:

MISSING! PREGNANT CAT.
Grayish brownish with black stripes
Big (PREGNANT) belly
Screeches a lot

Smelly
If found, please call 503-234-9999

Martha thrust a helmet onto Anand's head while she talked.

"Okay, Sanjay. This is my friend Fern's bike but she's gone all summer so she said you could use it." Anand watched his brother's face for signs of objection to the sparkly blue-green bike.

Sanjay glared at her.

"It's not going to win you the Tour de France, but it will get you to the swimming pool for six weeks," said Martha.

"And this one is for you, Anand! It used to be mine."

Martha wheeled out a purple bike with streamers and a basket.

Anand nodded. "It doesn't matter, Sanjay. We don't know anybody here anyway." Martha didn't give Sanjay any more chance to complain. At that moment, Auntie Fran came out and hopped on her bike.

"Ready, guys?" she asked.

Martha answered by speeding off down the driveway. They hurried after her.

———

Since Anand wasn't tall enough to hang the signs up, Martha made him carry the staple gun. The metal in the hot sun almost burned his fingers and the extra staples in his pocket were poking his leg. He wished they'd hurry up so they could get to the swimming pool and plunge into cool water.

But Martha was going crazy with the sign-hanging. She wanted them plastered everywhere. They'd ride a block, stop, hang a sign, hop back on the bikes, and ride another block. It wasn't until Anand caught a glimpse of bright blue water behind a fancy iron fence that he realized Martha had been leading them in the direction of the pool all along. Martha stopped them at the bike rack and he happily took the staples out of his pocket as Martha and Sanjay locked up the bikes.

The pool was packed with kids—kids splashing, kids on floaties, kids with pool noodles, kids in life jackets, kids walking along the deck as fast as they possibly could without having a whistle blown at them for running, kids launching themselves off the diving board, and kids leaping out over the water clutching a Tarzan rope and letting go to splash into the water.

Once they got inside, Martha dragged Anand to the nearest lifeguard. "My cousin needs to get his swim test," she said. She turned to Anand. "You think you can swim the length of the pool?" He nodded nervously. It wasn't the swimming he minded. It was the idea of someone watching him swim. He hopped into the water.

He easily crawl-stroked the length of the pool, hopped out, and shook the water out of his hair and ears. The lifeguard put a slick plastic purple band on his wrist, which meant he wouldn't need Auntie Fran to stay in the pool with him.

"Nice job!" said Martha, giving him a high five.

"That would have been humiliating if you failed, huh?" said Sanjay.

"Ignore him," said Martha.

Anand pointed to the line for the Tarzan rope. "Can we?"

She nodded.

There was a line of maybe a dozen kids waiting to swing on the rope. The three of them joined it.

When they got to the front of the line, Martha went first. She'd obviously done it before. She stepped up on a platform and a lifeguard handed off the rope. She clutched the rope and launched herself away from the platform. At the widest part of the swing, she let go and hit the water with a mighty splash.

"Me next!" said Sanjay, stepping in front of Anand. The rope swung back and the lifeguard caught it for Sanjay.

Then Sanjay swung like he'd done it a thousand times before, even though he hadn't.

Anand took a deep breath and stepped up onto the platform. He took the rope from the lifeguard and launched himself out over the sparkling blue water of the pool. He felt like everyone was watching.

Now? Now? Now? he kept asking himself. When to let go? He didn't know how long he could hold on. Then suddenly, he couldn't. At the widest part of the swing, he slid down clumsily, the rough rope scraping his belly. He hit the water and came up gasping. He swam to the side without looking around to see how many people had seen what happened. When he got out of the pool, he kept his head down so he wouldn't meet Martha's gaze. His belly was burning from the rope, and even worse, from the chlorine stinging the raw mark the rope had left.

"Are you okay?" Martha asked.

He didn't answer.

The kid who had been next in line now swam up behind him. "Nice one," he sneered.

"Almost as bad as the first time you tried it, *Winston,*" said Martha coolly. "Didn't the lifeguards have to come in after you?"

His mouth dropped open then closed again, and he swam away. "Don't worry about Winston Cleary. He's a big jerk," Martha assured him. "Want to try again?"

Anand shook his head. Not only did he not want to try again, he wished to be magically transported to the bottom bunk of Martha's house so he could close the curtains and stay there for the rest of the visit.

He could feel Martha staring at the rope burn on his stomach.

"Hey, that happened to me the first time I tried the rope swing, too. But I didn't get a scratch like that because I had a one-piece on."

Anand didn't answer her and kept on staring at the rope swingers. No one had any trouble except him.

"You need a hug?"

"No!" he shouted.

"Okay, okay," she said, putting a hand on his shoulder and guiding him to the open swim area. "Come on, let's go splash around."

Anand splashed Martha so ferociously the lifeguard blew a whistle at him. They both climbed out and sat on their towels. Anand knew he was pouting, but he didn't care. He was watching his brother perfectly execute the Tarzan leap over and over.

"You need more arm strength, I think," said Martha in her grown-up voice. "I could help you with that, if you want."

"How?"

"I can make you a fitness plan. I'll have you swinging like Tarzan in a few weeks," she said. "You think about it. I know I'd make a great personal trainer."

He didn't answer. It just sounded like a chance to get bossed around more.

8

THE AMUSEMENT PARK

"Saaaaanjay!" Martha's voice came through loud and clear from the bottom of the stairs.

Sanjay jerked upright, bashing his forehead on the attic rafters. Oof. He closed his eyes tight and put his hand to the tender spot. Hopefully he hadn't hit it hard enough to get a goose egg that would need explaining. He quickly fumbled for the envelope full of cash and touched the edge of it, just to reassure himself it was still where he'd hidden it, then rushed out of the crawl space.

"Be right down!" he called back.

"We're going to be *late!* There's going to be a *line!*" Martha shot back.

He came out to the top of the stairs.

"What were you doing in Mom's office?"

"Uh, looking for some tape. One of my magazines tore."

"Magazines are not important right now. We gotta go."

"I'm coming! Geez!"

They were one week into the visit and there was still no sign of Mama Cat. And no sign whatsoever of Martha giving up on the Forty-two Days of Fun List. So, a few minutes later, they were on their bikes, pedaling along a trail beside the river. Sanjay could hear the amusement park before he could see it. The rumble of metal wheels on rails told him there was a roller coaster, and a pretty good one judging from the sound of the screams. They came around a bend and he could see the midway and the top of the Ferris wheel.

He'd been to bigger amusement parks back home in Minnesota. Every summer, as a reward for good grades on their report cards, his mom and dad drove two hours to take them to a giant park where they spent the whole hot sticky day on thrill rides until practically the whole family got sunstroke. But he had to admit it was pretty great to live so close to one you could bike there.

They fought their way through the crowd to the ticket booth. The smell of caramel corn and hot dogs filled his nose.

"Here's money for some ride bracelets," said Auntie Fran. "You guys have fun and I'll be by the river with my knitting and my book. Find me when you're done. But no later than four p.m., please."

"Got it," Martha said, fiddling with her watch. "But before we split up, can you check your phone and see if anybody called about Mama Cat?"

Auntie Fran pulled her phone from her pocket. "Nope, nothing yet."

"Are you sure you want to do this today, Martha?" asked Anand. "We could search some more instead."

Sanjay slugged him in the arm.

Martha shook her head. "We can do that later this afternoon. We *have* to get through this Fun List. I'm not going to make this the vacation where all we did was hunt for a cat." She looked like she was tearing up again. But then her expression shifted from sad to determined. Good. Sanjay wanted to do something other than watch Martha cry.

"We're going to take a geographic approach to the park," she said. "We'll start with some of the tame rides, then hit some games. Then lunch. Then thrill rides. Then the best ride for last, the Looping Thunder. Then mini golf."

They set off. First stop was a huge slide where you sat on a rug to slide down. Pretty lame. Then the Tilt-A-Whirl. Then some ride shaped like a frog that shot you straight up into the air. By the time they stumbled off that one, Sanjay had that excited and out-of-breath feeling you get from nonstop fun.

"Bumper cars next," Martha said.

Sanjay eyed the bumper cars for a moment before deciding on the blue one with a white racing stripe.

"This is a good arm workout for you!" Martha shouted at Anand as Sanjay plowed his car into Anand's.

When the bumper cars came to a stop, they found a picnic spot and threw down a blanket. Martha handed out berries, cheese sticks, avocados, some sort of brown rice salad that Sanjay didn't like, and a few hard boiled eggs.

Sanjay noticed his brother eyeing the concession stand. Anand leaned over and whispered in Martha's ear.

She nodded, then reached in her pocket and handed him a five-dollar bill.

Sanjay wished Martha and Auntie Fran would stop buying them things.

Anand came back with a huge coil of purple cotton candy perched atop a narrow paper cone. He offered it around. When it was gone, they lay on the blanket and watched the crowd.

"Look at all the babies!" Martha cried. "They're all cheeks and eyes and drooly chins—I can't stand it! I keep telling my mom and dad to have another baby."

"Really? I don't know why you want a brother or sister so bad," said Sanjay. "It's just a lot of trouble."

Martha clamped her hands around Anand's ears and kissed his cheek. "I won't have you talking like that in front of your wonderful brother. You don't know a good thing when you see one." Anand shook himself free of her.

"Be careful what you wish for," said Sanjay.

Anand looked at Martha and said, "He sounds just like our dad."

Martha pulled out her notebook. Probably checking off the amusement park on that precious list of hers. But no, it looked like she was drawing something. After a few minutes, Martha showed him her picture: a baby eating a huge cone of cotton candy.

Sanjay rolled his eyes.

"Ready for more?" asked Martha. The boys sprung up in response.

Martha led them to a ball-tossing game. To win a prize, you had to sink a ball into a ring that was floating in a pool of water. Mostly, the prizes were lame stuffed animals, but some were actually pretty good. There was even a huge squirt gun. Martha dug into her pocket and paid for a round.

Sanjay stood back, watching.

"Don't you want to try?"

"I don't have any spending money," he said, trying not to look at Anand.

"Didn't your parents give you any for the trip?" asked Martha.

"They probably forgot. They were in a hurry."

"I can spot you," said Martha.

"I don't want to play," he snapped, scratching his suddenly itchy right hand.

"Well, Anand then," said Martha, neatly sinking a ball into a ring floating on top of a pool of water. She collected her prize of three jelly bracelets.

Anand stepped forward to toss a ball. He overshot the pool entirely and the ball bounced onto the ground.

"Good try," said Martha. "You just need more practice."

Anand looked embarrassed and didn't say anything.

"Come on," said Sanjay, tired of holding still. "Let's do some more rides. How about that big Screaming Hawk spinning thing?"

"No," said Martha, matter-of-factly. "We're doing the Cheery-O next."

"Come on!" said Sanjay. "Do I ever get a chance to choose something we do? Anand, what do you want to do?"

"I dunno."

"Listen," said Martha, impatiently. "I've been here before. I know the best things to do."

"Just because it's something *you* want to do doesn't mean it's the best thing." He needed to stand his ground on this one. Thrill rides were really important.

But watching Martha cross her arms and clench her teeth, he remembered that she was ready for *every* battle.

"I'm going on the Cheery-O. Are you coming?" she asked.

"If I come, can we do the Screaming Hawk right after that?"

Martha blew an angry puff of air through her nose. "Fine, but you're ruining the plan," she said.

The Screaming Hawk was worth it. Feeling the pressure of the harness holding him in but the force of the ride trying to launch him into the sky, Sanjay was vaulted into the air by a huge mechanical arm, then spun around until it felt like his brains were going to seep out his ears. When they all stumbled off, Sanjay grinned at Martha.

"See? So fun," he said.

Martha just grabbed his hand and pulled him ahead. "Now it's roller-coaster time!"

Scream Mountain was the biggest thrill ride in the park. You started up by climbing at a ninety-degree angle and then plunged, looped, and twisted. It looked amazing. Sanjay eyeballed the wood cut-out of a kid. It had lines marking the height requirement.

"You can't go on this one, Anand," he said. "You're too short."

"Yes, he can," said Martha. "I brought him my old high tops that have lifts in them," Martha said, starting to rummage in her backpack. That's when Sanjay noticed his brother's face was motion-sick green. Why hadn't he remembered that Anand needed to take it easy on rides—

Too late! Anand pivoted to the side and vomited on the asphalt. There was a considerable amount of purple cotton-candy matter in it.

Martha jumped back, then shrugged. "It wouldn't be a trip to the amusement park without somebody barfing," she said.

Sanjay rolled his eyes. "And that somebody is usually Anand."

Already, a park employee was coming over with a clean-up kit.

"Well, time to go home, then," said Martha.

"No way! What about Scream Mountain?!" Sanjay protested. But by now Anand was crying.

"Sanjay, your brother is covered in his own puke. Have a heart."

"I'll get a heart when he gets some guts."

"Let's go find my mom," said Martha firmly.

9

THE FARM STORE

A nand was dreaming about dinosaurs. He was crouched, hiding among some thick jungle foliage, watching two big T. rexes battle each other. The action was jerky, almost like stop-motion animation. But something wasn't right. The monstrous creatures didn't sound the way he'd always imagined them sounding. They weren't roaring. They were, well, squawking. And one of them was shouting his name, "Anand! Anand! *Ba-gawk!*"

Anand tried to concentrate on the squawks, tried to get them to make sense, but his mind was slowly sucked away from the dinosaur fight and into the bottom bunk of the guest bedroom of his aunt and uncle's house. From the open window came a breeze and the sound of chickens going "ba-gawk." And Martha loomed over him, whispering his name, "Anand! Anand! Wake up! It's time for your workout."

He groaned.

"Shh! You'll wake up Sanjay. Come on." She grabbed his T-shirt and pulled him out of bed.

His eyes barely open, he followed her outside.

"Let's find something we can use as a barbell," Martha said.

"Don't remember agreeing to this," Anand complained.

"You're only here for another five weeks. If you want to swing on the rope, we've got to get you strong, quick."

She grabbed a big shovel and laid it out on the patio.

"Okay, bend your knees and grab the shovel like a barbell, then lift it to your knees, bend at the elbows and lift it over your head, and then ease it down again," Martha instructed while demonstrating.

Anand picked up the shovel and lifted it over his head.

"My arms are shaking!" he cried.

"Good," said Martha. "That means it's working. Now do that fifteen more times."

Hours later, Anand got into the car for a trip to the grocery store. He was tired, and his arms were quivering, but he did feel a tiny bit stronger.

He stared out the car window, imagining Tarzan ropes hanging from every tree they passed, mocking him. The trees were much bigger and taller here than at home in Minnesota. As they drove on, he started to pay more attention to the view out the window than to the memory of his unwanted personal trainer. There were flowers he'd never seen before, and some big green plant everybody had in their yards that looked like it was from another planet, with clusters of bright lime-green flowers all over. His mom would love them, he thought.

But he didn't want to start thinking about his mom too much. He focused out the window again. A white cat sat crouched in a flower bed. In Minnesota, cats stayed in the house. And you'd never see a car with goats in the back like that station wagon. Wait!

"Stop!" he shouted. Auntie Fran slammed on the brakes.

"What is it?" she asked, craning her neck to look in the back seat.

"Goats! Goats!" Anand shouted and pointed. "In that car!"

Sanjay said, "They can't be goa—" Then he saw them and shut his mouth. In the wayback of the station wagon next to them were two goats frolicking, as much as it was possible to frolic in such a small space.

"Oh, for heaven's sake," said Auntie Fran.

"Told you so! Told you so!" Anand shout-chanted.

Martha yelled, "Follow that car!"

"Okay, since it's unanimous. But everybody needs to stop yelling." Aunt Fran let the goat car pull ahead of her and moved into the lane right behind it. At each stop, they waved their arms wildly and the goats stared out of the back window at them.

Finally, the goat car pulled into a small parking lot.

"Of course!" shouted Martha. "They're going to the farm store! The farm store is on the list!"

Aunt Fran parked, and everyone piled out. The woman

from the station wagon said, "Do you guys want to meet the goats?"

"Yes! Please!" said Anand.

Martha was bouncing up and down again and bumping into him, but this time he didn't care.

The woman fumbled around in the back seat, and finally two little goats, no bigger than Martha's dog, hopped out onto the gravel of the parking lot and strained against their leashes to trot over to him.

"Meet Poppy and Bubbles," said the woman.

"Are they babies?" Anand asked.

"They're about two years old. They're pygmy goats, so they'll stay this little. Here, hold out your hand," she said to Anand. She gave him a few pieces of diced carrots from the pocket of her overalls, and in a flash the goats were snuffling out of his hand. He forced himself not to pull his hand away, even though their wet tongues tickled his palms.

"Poppy and Bubbles love coming here," the woman said.

And for the first time since getting off the plane, Anand thought, *Me too.*

"Come on, you guys," Martha said. "We have to see the chicks." She led them past shelves stacked with jars, bottles and tubs, sacks of food, gardening gloves, and shovels, toward a strange peeping sound. At the back of the store were dozens of cages with hundreds of chicks. Fuzzy yellow chicks, fuzzy black chicks, fuzzy speckled chicks—they were surrounded by the din of tiny peeping voices. They went from cage to cage, Anand trying to read the weird breed names aloud: Buff Orpington, Speckled

Sussex, Rhode Island Red, Gold Laced Wyandotte, Australorp, Barnevelder, Plymouth Rock, and the Polish, which were Anand's favorite—a dozen little chicks wobbling around with tiny domes of bushy feathers on top of their heads. He pressed his nose to a cage and reached in a finger, but the chicks skittered away from him.

"Anand, come here," Martha was standing near a tall display of huge and heavy-looking bags stacked on a wooden pallet.

"What?" he asked.

"Strength training. You get to carry one of these out to the car."

"But what are they?"

"Chicken food. We're almost out."

Martha picked up one of the gigantic bags and heaved it into Anand's arms. His legs almost gave out from under him.

"Uh, Martha," he heard Sanjay say. "He's definitely going to drop that."

Anand hugged the bag tight to his body. The top corners were blocking his view, and the bottom of the bag was bumping to his knees. He knew it was too much, but he didn't want Sanjay to see he couldn't do it.

"I can't see," was all he said.

"Don't worry! I'll guide you."

He felt Martha's hands on his shoulders and she slowly pushed him through the store to the check-out counter.

"Do you want to put it down while Mom pays?" Martha asked.

His arms were burning, but he was afraid if he put it down, he wouldn't be able to pick it back up again.

"No," he said tightly, his breath partly held.

"Are you sure you've got that, Anand? That's twenty-five pounds," said his aunt.

He let the bag sag down a little so he could at least see where he was going.

When Auntie Fran was done paying, he said to Martha, "You first."

"Right, I'll open the trunk for you."

But just as they were walking out the door, Anand ran right into Martha's back. She'd stopped walking. He lost his grip on the bag and twenty-five pounds of chicken food hit the cement floor of the store. The bag burst open, scattering bits of grain everywhere. He wanted to disappear.

"Told you so," Sanjay said to Martha. But she wasn't listening. She stood frozen, with her hand pointing up at a poster on the wall. It said: *ALERT. COYOTES SPOTTED IN SOUTHEAST.*

"What...what if..." Martha stammered, her face completely white. "What if the coyotes find the kittens before we do?"

"Oh dear," said Auntie Fran.

"Oh," said Martha, her eyes filling with tears. "Now we *really* have to find Mama Cat! We just have to find her!"

Anand pressed his tongue hard to the top of his mouth so he wouldn't cry, too.

"Martha, try not to worry," said Auntie Fran. "Cats are pretty good at taking care of themselves and their kittens."

"But, Mom! Coyotes!"

"I know, Martha, I know. But let's just get this mess cleaned up and get going."

Anand couldn't get out of there fast enough.

10

THE RISING TIDE

I t rained the first few days of July, and by the fourth, when they were supposed to leave for the beach, Sanjay had begun to lose hope of ever seeing the sun again.

He was carrying this backpack downstairs to the mostly loaded car when he heard Martha, sounding upset. He paused on the stairs to listen. Anand bumped into the back of him. Sanjay turned and put his finger to his lips.

"We can't just leave!" Martha pleaded to Auntie Fran. "She's out there! Those kittens are out there!"

"Martha, we've already talked through this!" Auntie Fran sounded exasperated.

"I can't go! I'm *not* going! All the neighbors are going out of town, too! There won't be anyone to look out for her!"

"Martha, it's too late to cancel the beach house. The boys want to go to the ocean. Mama Cat is perfectly capable of taking care of those kittens. *If* they've even been born yet. We've got signs up. I really don't think there's anything else we can do."

"Yes, there is! We can cancel the trip and keep looking! Coyotes, Mom!"

Sanjay was pretty sure Martha was crying.

Anand leaned in and whispered in Sanjay's ear, "I don't think we should go either."

"Shut up about it," Sanjay hissed.

Aunt Fran sighed. When she spoke again, her voice was softer.

"Martha, I get it. But it's just one night. We've looked everywhere. We just have to wait for someone to call us."

"What if they call while we're at the beach? Can we come home if someone finds them?"

Aunt Fran sighed again. Her sighing sounded exactly like his mom's. It must be a family trait.

"Yes. Fine. If someone finds them, we can come home early."

Sanjay was relieved. The ocean was so different than the mosquito-infested lakes in Minnesota where their grandpa took them fishing. He couldn't wait. It was the thing they had most looked forward about this trip. And he was pretty sure they were never going to find the kittens anyway.

Hoping to put an end to the discussion, Sanjay started down the stairs again. He found Martha and Aunt Fran in the kitchen, hugging. But Martha still looked tense.

As the car crawled through holiday traffic, Sanjay sat in the back seat with his bicycling magazines and catalogs. He wanted to research his top three models and finally decide which bike to buy with the envelope full of cash that was still stashed in the crawl space. He'd probably need all of his saved-up birthday money, too. But it was hard to concentrate with Charlie the dog sitting on his feet and Anand taking all his elbow room.

Martha studied a map, her knitting lying untouched on her lap. She sniffled occasionally. Anand stared out the window until his head flopped over, asleep. Sanjay figured that was for the best; less chance of car sickness.

After almost two hours on a winding road lined on both sides with miles and miles of forest, they left the highway and turned into a neighborhood. They crested a hill and the next right turn made Sanjay gasp.

There it was, the Pacific Ocean: big white-capped waves crashing onto a vast beach under a blue sky filled with puffy white clouds. Sanjay's entire body relaxed. They had made it to the ocean. He shook Anand's knee to wake him, then rolled down his window.

"Smell that?" Martha asked. "Salty sea air!"

Both boys took a deep breath through their noses. Sanjay had never realized that salt had a smell, but here it was.

The car rounded a sharp bend and the view of the ocean disappeared.

"We're here," said Uncle Marshall, pulling into a gravel driveway. Martha started bossing them around again. Sanjay barely had time to open his car door before she was loading them with luggage. "It's part of your workout, Anand," she said. They threw the bags into the house and Martha barked at them to follow her.

Sanjay objected, "Can't we see the house first?" He had

never stayed in a rented beach house before and wanted to pick his bedroom before Anand could.

"Nope! Ocean first!" said Martha and strode off.

"Be back by four!" Aunt Fran shouted after her. Martha raised her watch hand into the air. Sanjay sighed.

He and Anand followed her down a long quiet road hemmed in by huge trees covered in moss. He could already hear the roar of the ocean and was impatient to see the crashing waves.

"How long does this road take to get to the beach, Martha? The ocean sounds like it's right here," Sanjay asked.

"You have to walk around this little wood. This is a state park. Trust me, I studied the map."

After about five minutes of walking, the road finally spit out into a picnic area. Striding between picnic tables crowded with vacationers, Martha led them to the edge of a bluff that overlooked the beach below. Sanjay stopped to look at the ocean, but before he had a chance to check out the view, Martha gave him a slight push on the shoulders and yelled, "Onward!" Then she passed him and walked to the edge of the bluff, bent her knees deeply, and led the way down. After a few steps, Sanjay found he had to sit and scoot his way down. He glanced back and saw that Anand was sliding on his butt, too.

"Martha, are you sure this is the best way to get to the beach?" yelled Sanjay.

"Sure, why not?" she said, and then lost her footing and slid—uncontrolled and shrieking with delight—all the way to the bottom. Sanjay and Anand landed within a few feet of her.

They stood in a small cove between two bluffs that jutted into the ocean. A salty mist cooled Sanjay's face and the roar of the ocean filled his ears.

"Let's pick out the best spot to watch the fireworks from," said Martha.

"Are you sure this is where the fireworks will be?" Sanjay shouted. The strip of beach was only a few feet wide. This couldn't be the place. But Martha had already started running along the narrow strip of sand between the bluff and the crashing waves. The boys chased after her.

"Martha! Wait!" Sanjay shouted.

With the roar of the ocean and her running so far ahead, she must not have heard him because she didn't answer. But now she was stopped and bent over, her hands resting on her knees, examining something.

The boys caught up. Martha pointed down at a small pool that had three bright orange and very fat starfish hanging out in it.

Anand gasped. "Can I touch one?" he asked.

"Of course," said Martha. "But be gentle."

Anand poked at the biggest starfish.

Sanjay leaned over and ran a finger along the smallest one. It felt firm and rough. He looked up again at the rising surf, then down the beach. There was nobody else around.

"Hey, Martha," he said, eyeing the shrinking span of sand. "I don't think this is where the fireworks will be. The beach isn't big enough."

"Huh?" she said. She looked out at the water and frowned. She checked her watch.

"Uh-oh," she said. She looked up at the bluff they were standing below. "It's almost high tide. This cove disappears at high tide."

"Disappears?" asked Anand, confused.

Sanjay looked at up the cliff, too. There were obvious watermarks high on the bluff face. At high tide, this entire section of beach would be under water.

Sanjay grabbed Anand's hand and they ran back the way they had come, but it was obvious that the embankment they'd slid down was too steep to climb back up.

There were just a few feet of beach left. The waves were licking their ankles and Sanjay's T-shirt and shorts were wet from the spray. Martha took hold of Anand's hand and they ran ahead.

Sanjay's thighs started to burn from the strain of running in the loose sand. They were past the southernmost bluff, but the beach was still very narrow. Another steep embankment rose up ahead, with dense trees at the top, and Sanjay spotted a wooden staircase going up it. A trailhead! He pushed himself to run even faster and passed Martha and Anand shouting, "Follow me!"

He rushed up the decaying steps and turned around to make sure they were behind him. In a moment, they were all standing on the top step and watching the waves crash ever closer to them. They stared at each other, panting. Sanjay was sweaty and shaking.

"Now what?" asked Anand.

"Now we wait for the tide to go down and then find a way back to the beach house," said Martha.

"No," Sanjay' said. "This *is* the way back. We follow this trail."

"You have no idea where this goes," said Martha.

Sanjay yelled, "Neither do *you*. We're done listening to you. You got us into this mess! Here's what I know: if I hadn't found this staircase, we would have drowned! And I also know that this trail leads *away* from the ocean. Come on, Anand." He took hold of his brother by the shirt and turned to stomp off, barely in time to prevent Martha and Anand from seeing the hot tears that sprang to his eyes.

Sanjay kept picturing his mom's face if he had to explain something bad happening to Anand. Saying it was Martha's fault wouldn't cut it. He was the big brother.

The trail rose steeply and switched back across the hillside. The roots of the enormous trees stuck out all over the path. Sanjay shoved Anand out in front of him to be sure he wouldn't trip and fall down the steep hillside.

They came to a viewpoint that let them look all the way back down to the beach far below. Waves were crashing onto the beach even higher than where they had been admiring starfish.

The trail was more level now. Sanjay took the lead again.

"Can you slow down?" panted Anand. Sanjay slowed.

"I'm hungry," said Anand.

Sanjay stopped, turned around, and glared at him.

"What?" asked Anand defensively.

"What am I supposed to do about that?" said Sanjay. "We don't have any food."

"I know. I'm just saying."

"Well, tell Martha. It's her fault we're on a trail to nowhere with no food and no water."

"Listen!" said Martha. "I'm really sorry! I made a big mistake."

"I have to pee," Anand interrupted.

"We're in the woods, Anand," said Sanjay, throwing his arms wide. "Pee anywhere you want."

"Stay here, okay? Wait for me." Anand walked off to find a private spot.

Sanjay sat down on a fallen log at the edge of the trail. Martha cautiously took a seat a few feet over.

"Sanjay," she said quietly. "I'm really sorry."

"I know. And I'm really mad."

"I know," she said and went quiet again. Sanjay was strangely proud that his anger had made his cousin speechless.

He began to look around. This was unlike any woods he'd ever been in. The trees were four times the size of the trees he was used to seeing and absolutely everything was covered in thick green moss. The sunlight filtering through the canopy gave the light a green tint. On the ground were rotting stumps and ferns. The smell was a mix of salty ocean air and damp pine needles.

Sanjay finally took a deep breath.

"Wow," said Martha. "It's really pretty here."

Sanjay was about to lay into her that, yes, it *was* pretty here, though it would be nice to know exactly where *here* was, but just at the moment they heard Anand tripping his way back to the trail.

"I saw a huge slug! It was as big as my foot!" he said.

"Where?" said Martha.

"Over there where I was peeing. It got away, though," said Anand.

"Too fast for you, huh?" said Sanjay.

They set off again, slower this time, with Anand carefully scanning the ground and trees for more slugs.

Just as they were all drooping with hunger and fatigue, and after what felt like hours and miles of hiking, the trees began to thin out.

"Hey! This must be the road we walked in on," cried Martha.

Relief flooded through him. "See, told you that was the right trail," said Sanjay.

In another minute they came to the gravel driveway of the house. Auntie Fran rushed out to meet them.

"Oh, there you are!" she said. "We were worried sick!" Her tone turned angry. "Dad went down to the beach to look for you. What happened? You were supposed to be back almost an hour ago."

Sanjay pushed Martha by the shoulders to the front of their tired group. She had a lot of explaining to do.

An hour later, Sanjay was up to his elbows in dishwater. Martha and Anand were next to him, half-heartedly drying plates. Washing the dinner dishes was one of the consequences of the beach stunt.

"You're still mad at me, aren't you?" said Martha.

"A little," said Sanjay. His anger had spiked when his aunt and uncle explained that Martha had, in fact, almost killed them. The Coast Guard was constantly having to rescue clueless people from that cove at high tide. Then his anger had started leaking away. "But not too bad. I do get sick of you acting like you're in charge all the time and that you know everything."

"I'm not trying to. I just want to show you guys a good time. I'm trying to be a good host."

"But you know you're doing it, right?"

Martha sighed. "Yes, I guess so. Fern sometimes complains, too. Mom and Dad say I should get 'buy-in' from people instead of just telling them what to do."

"Good advice," said Sanjay. He wondered how many times Martha had been told this, and if she had ever really listened.

"What's 'buy-in'?" asked Anand.

"It means you should get people to agree with your ideas," said Sanjay.

"But I do have good ideas, right?" Martha pleaded. "You are having fun, aren't you?"

"Yes, but sometimes I want to decide for myself what to do."

"Okay, how about you can boss me around for the rest of the night?"

"That's a start. But don't think I don't see that you're *telling* me to boss you," he said and snapped her arm with the wet dish cloth. "First of all, you wash *and* dry. Then it's time to get some firewood down to the beach."

And for the rest of the evening, Sanjay was in charge. He led them to explore a new and improved way down to the water. It turned out that if they headed in the opposite direction from the way Martha had taken them, there was a perfectly easy way to get to the beach: just follow a narrow trail through a field of reeds and there you were. And now that the tide was going out, the beach was huge.

Sanjay decided where the bonfire should be, as close as possible to the place where the fireworks would be set off—for maximum noise—and directed her to carry camping chairs to the spot. By the time they got set up, the sand was crowded with families sprawled out on blankets or perched on driftwood logs, ready to watch the big show. When he settled into a lawn chair at sunset, he couldn't take his eyes off of the waves, rolling endlessly in and out. His auntie and uncle sat behind them. Anand and Martha were on either side.

As the sun dropped below the horizon, the waves disappeared into the darkness. When it was completely dark, the fireworks started. The show was nice and noisy, with booms so big he could feel his lawn chair shake on the sand. He could smell the slightly rotten-egg smell of sulfur. The ocean was the perfect backdrop for the display of bright, exploding colors. As the display rose to its big finale, huge cracks and explosions in the air stacked on top of each other, the display of sparks rising higher and higher in the sky. Sanjay almost forgot to breathe. Martha kept looking at him, so he flashed her a smile once to show her he wasn't still mad. He glanced at Anand and saw awe in his face, too. They exchanged huge smiles before turning their faces back to the sky.

11

THE CAT PEOPLE

As Sanjay had predicted, nobody called about the kittens while they were at the beach. And back in Portland, day after day, there was still no sign of Mama Cat. Martha insisted that they plow ahead with the Forty-two Days of Fun List, so they went to the zoo and saw polar bears, giraffes, and big cats. They went to the Children's Museum, which Sanjay found unbearably boring. They trampled the backyard with soccer games and water fights. The boys tried to show Martha how to play cricket, but they only had a baseball bat to use, not a proper cricket bat. His dad promised he'd bring them both cricket bats as souvenirs from India. They mercilessly harvested the newly sprouted snap peas and were keeping a close eye on the raspberries, which would be ready for picking any day now. There had been lots of swimming, but scaredy-cat Anand had yet to give the rope swing another try, and they'd spent many long afternoons reading books in the hammock and the fort.

This mid-July morning, the weather was cloudy, and Sanjay sat staring out at a drizzly sky, poring over his cycling magazines. He narrowed his bike search down to two choices: the Laserspeed 600 or the Hash-Trail 1000. Anand was across the table from him reading *Treasure Island*.

Suddenly, Martha rushed in.

"Listen, guys," she said. "I had an idea about Mama Cat. We gotta go. Mom said she'd drive us."

Fifteen minutes later, they all piled out of Auntie Fran's car in front of an old brick building. The sign out front read *The Cat People* in gray letters superimposed over a big painted cat face, then in smaller letters: *Friends of Feral Cats.*

The lobby smelled like floor cleaner and damp cat. The walls were covered with big bright portraits of cats. Sanjay stopped to look at a painting of a dove-gray kitten when he felt something rubbing against his leg. It was an old black tom cat.

"Hi there," Sanjay said, leaning over to stroke him.

There was a patch of scarred skin where his left eyeball should have been. It looked really cool.

A quiet, weary voice drifted over from behind a long counter. "I see you've met Henry. He's the greeter. I'm Jacob."

Sanjay turned to see a skinny guy with an unsmiling expression. He had reddish hair and a baggy T-shirt that had the Cat People logo.

Sanjay could see why they made the cat the greeter instead of this guy.

"Well, Jacob—" started Aunt Fran.

"My pregnant cat ran away and we have to find her!" Martha broke in. "She had to have had the kittens by now! Where should we look? What should we do?"

Her cheeks were getting pink as she talked.

"Yes, we need a little guidance," added Aunt Fran.

Jacob frowned. "Come. I'll show you around and we'll talk."

Jacob started by showing them a room filled with cat toys and scratching posts, where at least a dozen kittens romped around ceaselessly. Sanjay sat down on the cement floor, worried the cats would be too skittish to let him touch them. But they weren't. Five of them trotted right up to him and climbed on him. The competing sensations of soft fur and sharp claws ran up and down Sanjay's bare arms.

"Sometimes people find a litter of kittens, but they can't, or won't, take care of them," Jacob said bitterly. "So we raise them here until they're big enough to be spayed or neutered and then adopted."

"Martha," Sanjay whispered. "Do you think someone might have already found her and brought her here?"

"Um, Jacob? Did anybody bring in a gray-striped mama and a litter in the last two weeks?" Martha asked.

"Lots of pregnant cats and litters. But we'll look at the adults next and you can check for yourselves."

Sanjay winced. A black-and-white kitten was clawing her way up his T-shirt. He handed it to Martha.

"It's kinda sad, huh?" said Anand, watching one small cat who was off in a corner by himself. "All of these kittens without homes. Without their moms."

Sanjay swallowed hard.

"Come on," said Jacob. Sanjay and the others eagerly followed him to a room full of sad-looking adult cats in large cages. Sanjay scanned carefully for Mama Cat, then met Martha's eyes. They both shook their heads.

"Are these cats up for adoption, too?" asked Auntie Fran.

"No. We only do kitten adoptions," Jacob said. "These cats needed medical treatment." His voice was flat, as if he'd had to explain this many times before and was bored with saying it. "We're trying to stop the feral cat problem from growing," he explained robotically. "Our volunteers trap wild cats and bring them in for spaying and neutering, and then release them again and make sure they get fed. We don't try to tame them." This surprised Sanjay. In his experience, grown-ups where always trying to tame wild things rather than let them be.

"Should we try to trap Mama Cat?" Anand asked.

Sanjay scowled at him. "Then how would we find the kittens, smart guy?"

"Oh right," said Anand.

"Why would a pregnant cat run away? Where would she go?" Martha asked.

"Well," said Jacob, directing his answer to Auntie Fran instead of Martha, "cats have an instinct to find a safe, quiet place to give birth. Maybe she doesn't like kids." Sanjay figured Jacob didn't like kids either. "Her instincts took over. I'd look around nearby, in all the sheltered places you can find."

"We've done that!" said Martha, sounding more upset. She took a step closer to him. Sanjay was afraid she was going to start yelling at this guy. "We have to find these kittens! They need us!"

Jacob looked annoyed and said, "Well, look again. Once the kittens are born, the mother moves them around to keep them safe."

All the energy in Sanjay's body shifted. He gave Martha a wide, hopeful grin. They could check all the places they'd already checked!

Martha took a breath like she was about to interrupt when Jacob went on pointedly, "Cats are excellent moms. She's taking perfectly good care of her kittens. She doesn't need help for that."

"That's a fascinating idea," said Sanjay. "There are creatures who don't need Martha's help."

"Ha, ha," Martha said dryly.

"But," said Jacob, "you do need to find the kittens and get them spayed and neutered so they don't end up having more kittens and making the feral cat problem worse. You might end up finding the kittens when the mom is not around."

"I hope so," said Sanjay. "She's not the friendliest cat. I can't imagine what she'd do if we tried to take her kittens."

"Sanjay, she's fine. She was just stressed," Martha looked annoyed with him.

"If that's the case, you'd want to live-trap her afterward. But I can send a volunteer team. That's a bit much to ask of kids," said Jacob.

"No, it's not," said Martha fiercely. "We can totally do that."

Back in the lobby, Aunt Fran filled out some paperwork to make them an official foster family. That way, when they found the kittens, the Cat People would help find homes for them.

Sanjay bent over to pet Henry the one-eyed tom again. He leaned into the stroking.

Anand nudged him. He was jabbing one of their missing cat posters into his ribs.

"Oh right," he said. "Hey, Jacob? Is there somewhere we could hang our poster?"

Jacob pointed to a large bulletin board and resumed his dejected posture behind the long counter. He seemed to be done talking.

On the way out the door, Aunt Fran stopped at a large donation jar and dug around in her purse. She gave each of them a five-dollar bill to drop in it. Sanjay took the bill reluctantly.

"Go ahead. They need all the help they can get," she said. He folded it dropped it in the mostly empty jar, thinking of the room full of motherless kittens.

Aunt Fran turned to Jacob. "Well, um, it was nice to meet you."

"No, it wasn't," said Martha, too loudly. Sanjay put his hands on her shoulders and steered her toward the door. She muttered, "Have you ever met such a creep in your—"

"Thanks for your help," Sanjay shouted.

As they walked out the door, Jacob called, "Let us know if you find them."

"*When* we find them," said Sanjay and Martha in unison, and the door slammed behind them.

12

THE WHEELBARROW

J acob, even though he was a creep, had given Martha new hope. Surely, they'd find Mama Cat in one of the places they'd already looked!

The second the car pulled into the driveway, Martha announced, "New search! Be stealthy! Listen for mewing!"

"You're yelling, Martha," Anand quietly pointed out and put his finger to his lips.

"Oh right," she whispered.

Her dad wandered out of the garage to meet them. "What's all this about stealth?"

"We have to search all over again!" said Martha, a bit quieter. "Mama Cat might be moving the litter around from place to place. Everyone split up and search all the places you did the first time."

Martha and Anand scoured the backyard. Martha's heart would make a small leap each time she spread out the branches of a hedge to peek behind or bent low to check under foliage. And each time the spot was bare.

Eventually, she and Anand collapsed in the grass, looking out expectantly for the others to come back, hopefully with a cat and batch of kittens in hand.

Her mother returned first, shaking her head slowly. Next came Sanjay, who raised his empty hands in a sad shrug. Next her father. "No luck," he said, "but I had an idea. Why not put Charlie on the job? Maybe he's a search-and-rescue dog."

Martha brightened.

"Why didn't I think of that?" And here she thought she was good in a crisis. She bolted into the house and returned with Charlie and the cat bed. She put his nose to the bed and said, "Find Mama Cat, find Mama Cat!" Charlie put his big nose to the ground and began sniffing. Martha got impatient when he stopped to pee. "Find Mama Cat!"

"First things first," said her dad. "That will probably help him concentrate."

Charlie made his way down the walkway, his nose following the path to the garden and the fort. He stopped and woofed at the closed garden gate. Martha opened it. Charlie went back to the fort and sniffed through the blankets of the fort. Then back out of the fort and around the garden.

"He's just going in circles!" Martha wailed. Both her parents shushed her. They all stood watching Charlie. She was about to give up hope.

Suddenly, Charlie stopped at the overturned wheelbarrow and stood frozen with his head bowed.

"Woof."

It was a quiet woof.

Martha ran over to the wheelbarrow and lifted it up. Underneath was a small lump of matted gray fluff. She gasped.

"Is that a dead rat?" asked Sanjay. Anand made a sound of disgust.

Martha held her breath and bent low.

It was a dead something. No wait. Its body was rising and falling ever so slightly. Martha gasped as she realized what she was seeing.

"A kitten!" she whispered and looked up at her mom, her eyes full of tears.

"Hold on, Martha." Her mom bent low and carefully scooped up the gray-striped fluff ball.

"Is it...?" Martha hated saying "it," but she didn't know if it was a he or a she. And she couldn't even bring herself to say "dead."

"I think it's alive, but let's get inside and warm it up. Everybody get back in the house."

Once inside, Martha raced to the bathroom for a towel.

"Let's get a good look. It might need a vet right away," said her mom.

The kitten was impossibly small. It fit in Martha's mom's hand with room to spare. Its eyes were shut tight and there was yellow crust around them. Dozens, maybe hundreds of thoughts and questions circled around inside Martha's head. Was this for sure Mama Cat's kitten? Was she sick? Was she even going to live? Where were the other kittens?

She searched her mom's face for clues about how the

kitten was doing. Her mom's eyebrows were practically touching over her nose. Never a good sign. Her mom was handling the kitten as carefully as if she was made of wet tissue paper. She looked at each of the kids and said, "She needs to see a vet. I don't know if she's going to make it, Martha."

Martha felt the tears well up again. She looked to her cousins and saw that they both had tears in their eyes, too.

There was an emergency vet clinic across the river. They were very familiar with the place. About once a year Charlie ate a sock and sometimes it was touch and go as to whether or not he could poop it out on his own. One time he had actually needed surgery. Martha knew the doctors at the emergency vet were super smart. They could save the tiny kitty.

Still, it was a tense drive. Martha held the kitten, rewrapped in several silk cloths from her old dress-up box. Her mom thought silk was overdoing it a bit, but Martha insisted such a small kitty needed the softest swaddling, not some scratchy old towel. Besides, they were her silks. She didn't care if the kitty ruined them.

Nobody talked. The boys didn't even do any of their regular back-seat jostling and bickering.

Martha was relieved to see that the waiting room had just a few other people and pets in it. Hopefully the wait wouldn't be long. Her mom filled out some paperwork and a vet tech came out.

"Hi, there. I'm Oona. I need to take a quick peek at the kitten." Martha watched her face carefully, but couldn't tell what she thought of the kitty's chances. Oona looked up after her inspection. "I'll be back for her as soon as I can, okay?" she assured Martha. "We'll do everything we can to help her."

So the kitten was a her. Martha noticed that Oona had *not* said, "She'll be fine, don't you worry."

When Oona came back, everybody got up. But Martha's mom said, "You guys better wait here. There are too many of us for the exam room."

"Mom!" said Martha, louder than she meant to. "I have to be there!"

"It's okay, Martha," said Anand. "We'll wait here and you can go back."

The small exam room smelled of disinfectant. Oona put the kitten on a small scale to weigh her. "Eight ounces! So tiny!" How could something so tiny survive on its own for even five minutes? How long had she been under that wheelbarrow? When was the last time she'd even eaten?

Martha listened carefully to the conversation between her mom and Oona.

"When did you find her?"

"About forty minutes ago."

"Were you able to feed her?"

"No, we didn't know what we could give her and wanted to bring her straight here."

"Has she been awake at all? Any meowing?"

"Not really."

"Our first priority will be to make sure she gets some nourishment."

"What about her eyes?" asked Martha's mom. "She looks like maybe she has some kind of infection."

"First we'll worry about getting her some kitten formula. Once she's stable—*if* we can get her stable—then the doctor will check her over for everything else." Oona paused. "Sometimes, mother cats will abandon a kitten if she can tell that there's something wrong with it. She'll focus on taking care of the healthy kittens in the litter instead."

Martha gasped. "Are you saying Mama Cat *left her to die?*"

"Yes, it's possible. I'm sorry. I know it seems horrible, but it's part of a cat's natural instinct."

There was no holding it in, and Martha didn't try. She released a loud sob, and Oona handed her a box of tissues. Martha felt her mother's arm wrap around her shoulder.

"The doctor will be in as soon as she can."

The doctor came in a few minutes later and said they'd need to keep the kitten, at least overnight. "Then, if she's doing well, you can take her home and keep bottle-feeding her until she's well enough and old enough for solids."

"How old is she?" Martha asked.

"Based on her size and development, I'd guess about two weeks. Definitely young enough to still need her mom. Or a really good human surrogate mom." The doctor smiled at Martha. "We'll send you home with a bunch of information to study so you'll know how to take good care of her. But I need to warn you, lots of kittens in this situation don't make it. And if that happens, it's not your fault. You've given her the best chance possible by finding her and bringing her here."

Martha nodded, tears still leaking from her eyes.

When she opened the door back into the waiting room, the boys looked at her empty hands in horror.

"They need to keep her overnight," Martha explained quickly. "She might not make it, but they'll try."

It was another quiet car ride home.

13

MARTHA GETS FIRED

The next morning, Sanjay was in the basement folding laundry when they he heard Auntie Fran's phone ring. He raced upstairs to find her in the kitchen with her phone to her ear. From the serious look on her face, Sanjay could tell she was talking to the vet. Martha and Anand burst into the room, too, and Auntie Fran put a finger to her lips. When she got off the phone, she told them, "That was the vet. She's still not making any guarantees, but they had managed to get the kitten to take some fluids and formula. She needs to stay at the vet for at least a few more days."

Sanjay was surprised to discover how relieved he was.

"That's the good news," said Auntie Fran. Sanjay held his breath.

"The bad news is the vet thinks she's blind."

They all gasped.

It seemed weird that the vet didn't know for sure.

Weren't doctors, even animal doctors, supposed to know everything?

"She said animals adjust just fine to being blind," Auntie Fran went on. "But it might make it harder to find her a permanent home."

Martha squeaked to interrupt, but Auntie Fran cut her off. "I know your thoughts on this matter, Martha. No decision has been reached."

Hoping to avoid seeing another family fight, Sanjay asked, "Can we go to the pool today, then? If she's not ready to come home yet?"

"Great idea!" said Martha and her mom at the same time.

When they arrived at the pool, Anand looked nervously around. No matter how they changed the times and days they showed up to swim, Winston was there. And sure enough, here he was, right at the fence as they pulled up to the bike rack.

Winston threw Anand a nasty glare but didn't dare say anything. He never did while Martha was around. But a few minutes later when Anand lagged behind in the locker room, Winston was right there again.

"Hey, kid, let's go on the rope. Or are you too weak?"

Anand pretended not to hear him. With Martha as his personal trainer, he was building his strength, but he was not ready to try the Tarzan rope again. He held his breath, staring straight ahead as he walked past Winston out of the locker room.

Outside, he joined Martha at the end of the line for the diving board. He worked on perfecting his cannonball and his breaststroke. When no one was paying attention, he'd pull himself out of the pool over and over again to build up his arms.

The pool got very crowded after that, and a little later, Anand was relieved to see Winston's mom flagging him down and then heading toward the exit. When Winston was gone, Anand sat on the edge of the pool and watched the kids jumping off the Tarzan rope. Some kids gave a mighty push off the edge of the platform, some only a little nudge. Some let go of the rope at the last possible moment, others let go a bit too soon. After a few minutes, he found Martha in the shallow end, sitting in a patch of shade and soaking her feet.

"Go ahead. Give it another try," she said, pointing with her head in the direction of the Tarzan rope and gently splashing her feet in the water.

"Uh, no," said Anand.

"I think you're strong enough now."

"I don't feel any stronger yet," said Anand.

"You're just scared because of what happened last time. You have to try."

Anand glared at her. She jumped up.

"Come on. I'll stand in line with you," said Martha. She put her arm around his shoulder and together they moved stiffly toward the lineup for the Tarzan rope. Suddenly the sun was too bright, the cement under his feet too hot. He swatted Martha's hand off his shoulder. As he watched the kids jumping in front of him, he began to feel sick to his stomach. It felt like a dinosaur was trying to claw its way out. Only two more kids to go until it was his turn.

Martha leaned into his ear. "You can do it," she whispered.

It was too much. He turned to her and yelled in her face, "No, I *can't!*" and ran off to the locker room.

———

Martha sent Sanjay to the locker room after Anand and then waited at the bikes. She was kicking herself for going too far, pushing Anand too hard, too soon. But she'd been so sure that it was only a mental block. Under her program, she was certain Anand was strong enough to swing on that rope now.

"Martha," said her mother, who was sitting under a nearby tree. "Isn't this the second time the boys have told you you're being too bossy?"

"I was only trying to help," said Martha sulkily.

"Trying to help is great," said her mom, "but the way you're going about it isn't working. You're going to be a great leader someday, but you need to make sure people are willing to be led."

Just then the boys appeared in the doorway of the locker room and headed toward them. Martha stood up and opened her mouth.

Sanjay cut her off with a wave of his hand.

"Anand has asked me to ask you to not talk to him yet."

Martha slammed her mouth shut. There were eighty million things she wanted to say. It took all of her restraint to just nod. Then they all climbed on their bikes and started the silent ride home.

After dinner that night, Martha found Anand out in the hammock, still sulking. He was facing the arborvitae, watching the light of the setting sun flicker through the hedge.

She cleared her throat. He didn't turn around. "Anand, I don't want to bother you, but I just came out to apologize. I'm really sorry I pushed you to do the rope swing today."

He turned in the hammock glared at her. Sheesh, he wasn't going to make this easy.

"I should have let you make up your own mind if you were ready or not."

He gave a faint nod.

"And I'm really sorry."

He still wouldn't talk.

"I apologize."

More silence.

"It's just that I can see how strong you've gotten. Even if you can't, I can see it."

"Really?"

"Yes."

Silence again. Then finally, he spoke.

"I don't think I want a personal trainer anymore."

"Okay," said Martha. "I understand."

His body seemed to relax a bit, so she stayed silent for a while. Finally, she said, "Come on, let's go see if the raspberries are ripe."

Anand swiveled his head and narrowed his eyes at her.

"I mean, would you like to go check for ripe raspberries with me?"

"Sure," Anand said.

14

THE FUNDRAISER

The day the blind kitty came home was the hottest day of summer yet. They were camped out in the relatively cool basement, so the kitten wouldn't get too hot. She needed to be fed every two hours. She needed to be kept warm, but not too warm. She even needed her butt rubbed so she could pee and poop. Martha didn't mind tending to the kitten and holding her. In fact, she had a hard time wanting to do anything else. She'd created a new section of the notebook to carefully document kitten care.

The problem was they still had to find the mama cat and the rest of the kittens.

Stacks of paper and art supplies littered the cool cement floor of the basement. Martha leaned over her work, her hair falling in her face, while she put the finishing touches on her block lettering. She, Sanjay, and Anand were supposed to be making more fliers to post about the lost mama and litter. If you left the same old missing cat posters up for too long, people started to ignore them.

Martha looked up at Anand. He was feasting on raspberries they'd picked from the garden. Sanjay was holding the kitten in his lap, gently stroking the back of her neck.

"Are you guys still helping?" asked Martha.

"We're taking a little break," said Sanjay.

"Oh okay. If you think finding Mama Cat and her helpless kittens isn't important, I understand."

"I'm starving," complained Anand, ignoring her guilt trip.

"Me too," said Sanjay. "And I'm thirsty. It's so hot!"

Martha sighed. They were always starving. "Let's go upstairs and get some food. And I think we have some sun tea left."

But the pitcher in the fridge had only a few drops left. "Dad must have gotten to it," said Martha, drinking the last trickle straight from the pitcher. "You know what we should make? Lemonade!"

"Aw man! That would taste so good. I bet any kid who had a lemonade stand today would make tons of money," said Sanjay.

"If I made tons of money at a lemonade stand, I'd give it all to the Cat People," said Anand, who had carried the kitten upstairs and was gently stroking her gray head.

"What a great idea!" said Martha.

"Have you ever actually made money on a lemonade stand?" asked Sanjay skeptically.

"Yes, I have. I made twenty-one dollars at my last one," said Martha.

"Oh wow. I stand corrected. I'm sure twenty bucks will solve Portland's feral cat problem."

"I want to do it," Anand said stubbornly.

"Me too," said Martha. "Are you in or out, Sanjay?"

"Fine, add it to the list," Sanjay growled.

Martha picked up her notebook and together they sketched out a plan and supply list. They'd need lemons, sugar, cups, a table, a cash box, a sign and some markers, pens and a pitcher, and some chairs.

"I think we need all of today to get ready," said Martha. "Tomorrow's Saturday. We can catch all the garage-salers who need a cold drink."

"And we could put up the new fliers at the lemonade stand, too, so people could keep an eye out," Anand said.

"And we should make a sign that says all the proceeds go to charity," said Martha. "That will help sales."

Martha thought they should sell desserts, too, so they spent the afternoon in the scorching-hot kitchen baking cookies.

"Let's forget about the brownies," Sanjay said. "This is all I can take!"

"But—" said Martha. She was transferring the cookies to a cooling rack with a spatula. "I think they'll sell well!"

"Can I have a cookie?" Anand begged. He was lying on the cool tile floor. Sanjay handed a cookie down to him and then took two for himself.

"You guys! If you don't want to make more cookies, then you can't eat all the inventory!"

Sanjay paused from pouring milk and gave Martha a warning look. She sighed. She knew he meant that she was getting bossy.

"I'm going back down to the basement to cool off," she said.

"Oh good, so we're done now?" asked Anand.

"We still have to make the syrup and squeeze lemons, but I guess we can do that in the morning," said Martha. "And I was thinking Kitty can be our mascot! People are sure to donate if she's there."

"Are you going to think up a better name than 'Kitty'?" asked Sanjay. "Or is she going to suffer the same naming strategy as Mama Cat?"

"Very funny," said Martha. "But I guess you're right." She paused to think. "Willow. Her name is Willow. And she's going to help us sell loads of lemonade."

The next morning, Sanjay woke up sweaty. Even worse, he woke up with Martha's nose only inches from his own.

"Good morning," she said brightly. "Time to set up the lemonade stand."

Sanjay thought her voice was too cheery for the time of day and the circumstances.

He groaned and followed her down to the kitchen and watched her turn the cabinets inside out.

"What are you looking for?" he asked.

"A little lemon-juicer thingy. Mom!" she yelled before Sanjay could even reply.

Auntie Fran was downstairs. Martha poked her head into the basement doorway "Where's that little thing with the ridges for squeezing lemons?"

"If it's not in the kitchen, it's probably up in that box of extra kitchen stuff in the crawl space," she yelled back.

Sanjay let out a little gasp. "I'll go get it!" he said, and dashed up to Aunt Fran's office. Before searching for the kitchen supply box, he reassured himself that the envelope was still in place. Then he dug through some boxes until he found the lemon-juicer thing and delivered it to Martha.

Each of the billion lemons they bought had to be cut and then pressed and twisted to get all the juice out. The lemon juice stung a new fiberglass cut on Sanjay's hand. Martha didn't seem to enjoy this task either.

"Hey, Anand," she said, "I'll give you a dollar if you juice all the lemons."

"Two dollars. This can be my arm workout for today," he said.

"Fine," said Martha.

While Anand finished with the lemons, Sanjay and Martha dragged a table and a patio umbrella out to the edge of the lawn.

"Aw, man," said Sanjay, already sweating. "It's so hot!"

"I know," said Martha. "But hopefully this weather will be good for business."

"It won't be. It's too hot. No one will even be out."

"So optimistic," Martha said irritably. "I'll go get the cookies."

When Martha brought out the plate, Sanjay grabbed a cookie and wolfed it down without thinking.

"Hey! Don't eat all the stock! We made like eight-thousand cookies yesterday and we've got"—she quickly counted what was left on the plate—"eleven left."

"Which is eleven more than we'll actually sell," muttered Sanjay, his mouth still full of cookie bits. "I'll go get the sign."

They'd made the sign from a big piece of scrap plywood. Sanjay struggled with it. It was too large to pick up, so he held one corner and dragged it from the backyard to the front. "I guess I should have made Anand do this, for his workout," he said while propping the sign against the table. It read:

FERAL CAT LEMONADE AND COOKIES! 50 cents.

Then in smaller writing:

All proceeds go to the Cat People.

And of course, Martha had painted a large cat on the sign.

They taped up a few of their posters and Martha brought out the lemonade.

"We're ready!" said Martha with a little bounce. Sanjay couldn't believe she still had excitement in her voice.

They sat down in the sad sliver of shade provided by the umbrella and waited. Time ticked by, marked by the passing of cars that didn't stop for lemonade and the melting of ice in a big metal bowl. Anand was lying on the grass under the table, looking half dead.

When there was nothing but water left in the bowl, Sanjay asked, "Can we give up now?"

"No," said Martha and Anand in unison. "But," said Martha, "if you're bored, you can go get more ice. We used everything in the freezer. You'll have to go around the corner to the little store," said Martha.

"Fine," snapped Sanjay. Anything was better than sitting here. "Want to come along, Anand?" Maybe he could get Anand to carry the bag of ice.

"No, thanks," said Anand. Sanjay sighed and took a few dollars from the cash box and tromped off down the block. He bought a bag of ice. The cold bag was refreshing as it slapped against his leg, but it kept slipping out of his hand. He hoisted it up, hugging it against his chest, which felt even better, but the ice was melting so fast in the heat that his shirt was soaked by the time he got back to the lemonade stand.

"Any sales while I was gone?"

"Nope," said Martha.

"Nobody's going to come." He tore open the ice bag and picked up a cube, running it over his forehead and through his hair.

He heard a screen door slam across the street and turned around.

"Hi, Jim!" Martha shouted to her neighbor with a happy little wave. "Want some delicious lemonade?"

"Okay," he said. Martha shot Sanjay an I-told-you-so look.

Jim had gray hair and crossed the street slowly. He stopped in front of their sign and read it out loud. "'Feral cat lemonade.' Hmmm. Almost sounds like it's made by feral cats. Like it's their *urine* or something." He winked.

"Might prevent a few folks from stopping. But I'm feeling brave, so I'll try a glass."

Martha shrugged and poured him a cup. "It just means that we're doing it for the cats. They get all the proceeds."

"You know best," he said and took a big gulp. "It sure is tasty. I'll take one more cup, and you can keep the change." He handed Sanjay a five dollar bill.

"Wow, thanks!" said Sanjay.

"You haven't seen a litter of kittens around the neighborhood? Or a female cat with gray stripes?" said Martha.

"Nope. Sorry. But I haven't really been looking. You might ask Betty," he said, and pointed with his paper cup toward the house next to his. "She's a cat lover."

"Oh, great idea!" said Martha.

"Well, good luck. I'm going back to my air-conditioned house," said Jim, and he shuffled away. Sanjay wished he could go with him.

Martha poured a glass of lemonade. "I'm going to bring this to Betty and ask her if she's seen anything."

Sanjay snatched a cookie off the plate, stuffed it in his mouth, and watched as Martha carried the cup of lemonade to Betty's door.

A few cars drove by and slowed down but didn't stop.

Martha came back. "She's not home."

Another car drove by. Martha started jumping up and down and shouting, "LEMONADE! FERAL CAT LEMONADE!" and pointed to the sign.

Sanjay covered his face with his hands. The car drove on.

"I guess it's too hot," said Martha.

"Ya think?" said Sanjay sarcastically. He heard another

door slam. A different neighbor, wearing a big sun hat and sunglasses, walked across her lawn toward them.

"How's business?" she asked.

"Terrible," said Martha and Anand.

"That's too bad," she said. "Well, I'll take a glass of lemonade and a cookie."

"Great," said Martha while Sanjay got her order ready. "And have you seen any cats around the neighborhood? I'm missing my cat and her kittens."

"Hmm. I've only seen all the usual ones," she said. She complimented their baking and lemonade-making skills and hurried back to her house.

"There, we sold some," said Sanjay. "Can we please go inside now? I'm burning up out here."

"But, we've only earned six dollars for the Cat People," said Anand. "And no one has seen any sign of Mama Cat."

"I know," said Martha, the corners of her mouth turned down. "But I don't think staying out here longer is going to help."

"I guess not," said Anand. He crammed a cookie in his mouth and started gathering up the cups and other supplies. "This was a big waste of time."

"Told you so," said Sanjay, his spirits finally picking up.

15

THE GARAGE SALE

Anand had just finished his tenth push-up. He lay in the backyard, panting, his cheek pressed to the grass. He managed to get some kind of workout in almost every day. He mostly focused on lifting stuff and was always keeping an eye out for heavy things to use as weights. He now did all the chicken chores, including hefting the feed bags around. And the water buckets, which felt like they weighed about three hundred pounds. He figured he was almost ready for another attempt at the swinging rope. He only needed a few more workouts—and a day when Winston wasn't at the pool. He had only one week left to try.

Anand always tried to do his exercising when Martha was busy with something else: knitting, cooking, or writing in her notebook. Right now, she was in the basement, feeding Willow.

He was just sitting up, his breathing returning to normal, when Sanjay and Martha came into the backyard.

"What are you doing?" asked Anand.

"Getting you so we can go hang more posters. You're on stapler duty again.

Anand groaned.

They spent most of the morning driving around, plastering Southeast Portland with missing cat posters. He hoped this fresh batch of posters would finally mean that someone had spotted Mama Cat and the rest of the kittens. When they were finally done, Anand asked, "Auntie Fran, can we please take the long way home so we can see more of Portland?" He felt like all he ever saw was Martha's backyard and the swimming pool. And, of course, every telephone pole between the two.

"But—we have to get home to Willow!" Martha objected.

"Your dad has it under control, I'm sure," said Auntie Fran. "I think Anand has a great suggestion. Let's do it."

Auntie Fran drove them past the ghost building at the end of the Hawthorne Bridge (just lots of iron stuck together that looked like the shell of a building), and the rose gardens in the middle of a neighborhood full of fancy old houses (he could smell the roses, even from the car), then up Hawthorne with all its shops and cafes (and weird people), then Mt. Tabor park, which was built on top of an actual (but sadly dormant) volcano.

"Show them the house you and dad used to live in, Mom. You guys won't believe how tiny it is."

A few minutes later, the car stopped in front of a house about the size of a garage.

"It looks almost exactly the same as when we lived here," said Auntie Fran. "Look at all the fruit trees—

apples, pears, figs, plums, raspberries, even peaches. This is where I learned to love gardening." She drove down the block.

"Stop!" Martha suddenly shouted. Auntie Fran slammed on the brakes and Anand lurched forward against his seat belt.

"What?" she asked, looking frantically from left to right.

Martha flung out her arm and pointed up a driveway. "That garage sale has a tandem bike!"

"Cool!" Sanjay shouted.

"Oh Martha!" Auntie Fran's body slumped in the seat and she shook her head. "You almost gave me a heart attack. Don't you *ever* do that again."

"Sorry, Mom." Martha said. "I mean, may we please pull over and look for a few minutes?"

"Yes," sighed her mother. "But only because it will give my heart a chance to stop thumping."

They sprang from the car and stopped to admire the gleaming blue tandem bike.

"It practically looks brand new," said Sanjay, running a hand along the top bar of the bike.

The man running the garage sale was starting to pack everything up.

"Are you still open?" asked Martha.

"Well, sales haven't been great, so I was going to close up, but you guys can shop. I'll still take your money." He smiled.

There were loads of kid stuff. Anand saw some goggles and pool noodles and a beat-up crossbow with foam tipped arrows. He waggled some five-pound arm weights at Martha.

"How much are these?" he asked her.

"Ask *him*," Sanjay said, gesturing to the man. Anand scowled.

"How much for these weights?" he asked.

"Um, how about five cents each?"

Anand looked at Martha, disbelieving.

"Really?" Martha asked.

"Yup, the more stuff you guys buy, the less I have to haul away."

Martha turned to Auntie Fran. "Can we get them for Anand, Mom?"

"Sure. I think I can manage ten cents."

They huddled. "Let's look at *everything*. There could be some crazy-good deals," said Martha.

"Look!" said Sanjay. He was holding a rectangular wire cage with a metal handle on the top. "A cat trap!"

"Yup," said the man. "I used it to catch some nasty squirrels who were tearing up my yard, but you could use it for cats."

"Grab it!" cried Martha. "If we find the kittens first, we can use that to catch Mama Cat."

A screen door slam and Anand looked up from some comic books to see Winston coming out of the house.

Before Anand could think of what to say, Martha said, "Hello, Winston."

Anand clenched his jaw tight. He wanted to bolt for the car.

"Here," said the man, who must be Winston's dad, though he seemed too nice. "Hand me that trap for a minute. I'll show you how to set it." He demonstrated how to set the spring snap shut on the cat. "What do you guys need to catch a cat for? Did you lose one?"

"Yes," said Martha. "My cat. I had just got her and she was pregnant and she escaped. Now she's had the kittens and she abandoned one of them."

Winston made a little noise of surprise and concern.

"We have to find her and the rest of the litter. She's obviously a terrible mom. And she and the kittens need to be spayed and neutered," said Martha.

"What happened to the abandoned one?" asked Winston. No hint of the usual sneer in his voice. Weird. Anand thought maybe he was just putting on a show of politeness for his dad.

"We've got her. We're taking care of her, bottle-feeding her and everything. She's probably only three or four weeks old."

"Is that right?" said Winston's dad. "Sounds like a lot of work. You must really like cats."

Martha nodded.

"Well," said the man, "it just so happens I've been in the market for a kitten myself. Actually, I want to get one for Winston."

"Well," said Martha, "If we end up finding the litter..." Martha spoke slowly, looking at Winston.

"We could adopt one of them!" said Winston, finishing her sentence.

Anand poked her hard in the back. Martha slid her left foot back and stepped gently on his toes as a signal to stop.

"Well, yes," said Martha, hesitantly. "We'll need to find homes for them. And I guess you if have experience. There might be an application process. But we have to find them first. Hang on." She ran to the car and came back with one of the last fliers and handed it to Winston. "Please keep an eye out."

"I will!" said Winston.

Martha turned back to Winston's dad and pointed at the tandem bike. "Is *everything* a nickel?"

"Well," the man chuckled. "Considering you're hopefully giving me a kitten, how about you take the bike in trade? And if we don't find the kittens, well, we'll work something out."

Mouths wide open, Martha and Sanjay looked pleadingly at Martha's mom. Anand wanted her to say no just so they could get going.

"Can we please, Mom?"

"Please, Aunt Fran?" added Sanjay and Anand.

She nodded solemnly. "If it will fit in the car."

Winston's dad helped them take the front wheel off the bike and wedge it into the trunk. He even handed Anand a bit of twine and helped him tie the trunk shut with it.

Back in the car, Martha shook her head in disbelief. "Wow. Winston's dad is *nice*. Who would have guessed?"

"And Winston was nice," said Sanjay.

"No, he wasn't," said Anand. "He isn't."

"Well, he seems to be nice when there's talk of cats," said Martha. "If he can help find them and adopt one, I'm willing to forgive and forget."

"I'm not," said Anand.

16

ANAND AND ANDRE

The next day, just after lunch, Anand was sitting at the table eating a banana for dessert and watching through the window as Martha and Sanjay practiced riding the tandem bike together. Sanjay was in front. He could hear them yelling at each other through the open window. "No, this way!" "Okay, stop!" Each one seemed to be fighting to be in charge of where they were going and both of them looked frustrated. Anand shook his head. There was no telling how this fight would end. He popped his last bite of banana into his mouth and headed to the backyard for his workout, taking Charlie the dog and his new dumbbells along with him.

He could tell his upper body strength had improved. He'd lifted shovels, logs from the wood pile, buckets of water, bags of chicken feed, and even Andre the giant hen (who weighed more than he thought and squirmed like crazy). He'd done arm curls with gallon milk jugs, and practiced chin-ups using a step ladder and the branch of the pear tree.

It would be epic. He'd be Tarzan, swinging across a river of piranhas to rescue a baby from the jaws of a tiger on the other side, with Winston standing on the banks of the river, frozen in fear.

He set up the step ladder below the pear tree in the chicken yard and grabbed the branch with both hands. The chickens were scratching their way about the middle of the yard, looking for tasty worms to eat. He could still hear Sanjay and Martha shouting at each other from the street.

He took a few deep breaths before he began. When he'd first started using the pear tree for pull-up practice, he'd not been able to lift himself even an inch. His only goal was to hang there and tighten his muscles. After a few days of that, he'd slowly begun bending at the elbows. Now he could raise himself a few inches about ten times. Today, his goal was to touch his chin to the branch and do fifteen lifts.

By his twelfth pull-up, his arms were burning. He bent his elbows and lifted his feet off the ladder. Suddenly, Sanjay and Martha, still on the tandem bike, came barreling into the backyard.

"Sanjay, stop!" Martha screamed. "It's too fast! You're going to crash us!"

Sanjay steered them into the grass and the front handlebars jackknifed, catapulting them both off the bike and into the grass. Charlie started barking wildly and the chickens ran terrified from the scene.

Anand watched in horror as Andre, the giant hen, lumbered right into the step ladder, knocking it over. Anand lost his grip on the branch and crashed to the ground, his entire body weight landing on his right arm. Pain shot through all the way to his chest and when he tried to push himself up, the pain made him stop breathing. *This is what it feels like to break your arm,* he thought.

He screamed.

Martha rushed to his side. "Where are you hurt?" she said, hovering over him.

"My arm! I think it's broken." He looked down to find he was covered in dirt and chicken poop.

"I'll get Dad!"

In a moment, Auntie Fran and Uncle Marshall came running out. Uncle Marshall picked him up by the hips and set him on his feet. He winced as another surge of pain went up his arm and through his body. His legs almost gave out from under him.

"Let's get you to the hospital," said Auntie Fran.

During the endless wait in the emergency room, Martha tried to distract Anand with the story of a classmate in the first grade who'd broken her leg while trying to ride her bike over a haystack.

"Can you imagine breaking your leg when you were first learning? Geez, would you ever want to get on a bike again?" she said. But Anand could only focus on the pain. It was the worst he'd ever felt in his life. He glared at Sanjay, who seemed to read his mind.

"It's not my fault!" Sanjay protested.

"It kind of is," Martha said. "You were being too wild on the bike. Someone was bound to get hurt."

"It would be my fault if *you* got hurt, Martha. You were actually on the bike with me. But only Anand would break his arm because of a chicken. I can't be responsible for that."

"But you are," Anand growled. Suddenly a new horror struck him. "And you ruined my change for the Tarzan rope!" They were leaving for home in six days.

Sanjay started to protest, but just then a nurse came out to take him back to a room.

"You stay here," he snarled at Sanjay.

"Can I come?" Martha asked.

"Yes," said Anand.

The doctor came in and looked at his arm. "Forearms aren't supposed to be wavy," she said, her voice too cheery for Anand's liking.

He explained that he'd been hanging from a tree and a chicken had knocked his ladder over. The doctor raised an eyebrow.

"A chicken?"

"Yes, a big one. My brother scared them and they all ran at me. The big one knocked over the ladder."

"She's a Jersey Giant," Martha explained. "Big as a dog but a total, well, chicken."

"We'll need to get an X-ray. But it's certainly broken," the doctor said. "Better start thinking about what color cast you want."

"And then think up what flavor of ice cream you want

for dinner," said Auntie Fran. "I'm taking you out. That might cheer you up."

"Ice cream won't help," Anand pouted.

"Well, it's worth a try," Martha said. "And it's on the list."

17

ICE CREAM INTERRUPTED

Martha took a missing cat poster from the stack she kept in the trunk before heading inside the ice cream shop. Her mom and dad were standing on the sidewalk with Anand, who was now sporting a bright blue cast.

"I'll meet you in there!" she shouted. Inside the door was a big bulletin board. There were posters about yoga classes, guitar lessons, tarot readings (Martha really wanted one of these), and lawn-mowing services. She found a blank spot and pinned up her flier.

"Oh, did you lose your cat?"

Martha turned around. There was a familiar-looking woman standing at the back of the line which stretched all the way to the door. She was smiling, but looking worried for Martha.

"Yes, my pregnant cat ran away. She's had kittens by now. We found one of them that she abandoned and we're fostering her."

"Oh dear. I heard on the radio the other day that the feral cat problem is particularly bad this year. I'm considering fostering. We lost our cat a few months ago. It's been really hard on my son. It must be hard on you, too. Cats can be such members of the family."

"Oh, I'm so sorry," said Martha. She wondered if *knowing* that your cat was dead was worse than *wondering* if she was dead. "How old was your cat?"

"Oh, pretty old. We think about nineteen. My son grew up with him. He's about your age. You look familiar, by the way," said the woman.

"So do you! I'm Martha. Nice to meet you."

Just then Winston came out of the restroom and toward them.

"Martha! I was hoping to run into you at the pool today!" He turned to the woman. "Mom, this is my friend Martha."

Oh boy, she thought, *this is Winston's mom*. Who was she going to bump into next, his grandma?

"Yeah, well," said Martha. "We didn't make it to the pool. We got a little sidetracked."

Winston was waving his arms excitedly to interrupt. "I think I saw your cat!"

"What? Where?" said Martha.

"We were just by the park, and I saw her run up an alley a couple blocks from your house. Gray tabby, right?"

"Yes!" she shouted.

Just then the boys came in. When they saw who she was talking to, they looked shocked. Her parents were right behind them. Winston and his mom swiveled around to greet them, and Martha made overly smiley faces at the boys that she hoped told them to be nice.

"Winston saw Mama Cat!" said Martha.

"Ohhh!" said Sanjay. "Where?"

"Just a few blocks from the house! We gotta go look again, right now!"

"Are you all willing to skip ice cream?"

"Of course!" Martha shouted, then caught herself and looked at the boys. "I mean, are you?"

"Of course," both boys said together.

"I can come along and show you just where I saw her, can't I, Mom?

After a quick exchange of phone numbers, they set off in two cars, Winston riding with Martha and her dad, and the others following in Mrs. Cleary's car.

———

Martha looked anxiously out the car window. The sky was darkening with gray clouds. As they approached Martha's neighborhood, her dad started to drive slower. Cars were stacking up behind them. Winston pointed to a house with a rickety wooden fence, just a block and a half from Martha's.

"I saw her cross the street right here and slip under that fence!" said Winston.

"Dad! Turn down that street!" Martha glanced behind to make sure Winston's mom was following. Her dad stopped.

"I think we should get out and look around that yard," said Martha.

"Knock on the door first, and tell the owners what you're doing," said her dad.

But nobody answered their knock. A few fat raindrops started to fall. Martha turned and shrugged at her dad. Her dad pulled the car to the side of the road and Winston's mom pulled up behind him. Everyone was just getting out to help look.

"Let's go search," she said to Winston.

At the back of the driveway, right up against the garage, was an old canoe, flipped upside down to keep it from filling with rain. As they tiptoed toward it, Winston stumbled on a crack, lurched, and fell. A tabby cat shot from under the canoe, up the driveway and toward the street.

"It's her!" Martha shouted. She turned and ran after it. Martha saw the cat start to dart across the street just as a tiny electric car was coming. It was on a direct path to collide with the cat. Martha screamed, *"STOP!"* The car squealed to a quick stop and for a split second, she thought the cat was just fast enough to get clear.

She ran to the other side of the car. Mama Cat's hind legs were pinned under the front wheel.

"Back up!" she screamed at the driver. Hot tears were running down her face and her heart was pounding in her ears. The car slid back a few feet. Her dad was standing at her side. He took off his T-shirt, bent over, and scooped up the cat before Martha could get a good look. But she definitely saw blood. Too much blood. Her mom came and lifted her to her feet.

She heard the car door open and the driver say something, but she was sobbing too hard to understand what it was. Her dad was issuing orders. Her mom pushed her into Winston's mom's car, then got into her own car and drove off with Dad in the passenger seat holding Mama Cat. Martha tried to get out of the car to run after them, but Sanjay held her down.

18

THE LAST SEARCH PARTY

artha and the boys were in Martha's kitchen with Winston and his mom. Rain was now pounding against the windows, and Martha, slumped against the cabinets, could hear thunder in the distance.

"It seemed like it was just her legs," said Sanjay in a hopeful tone. This only made Martha cry harder. She couldn't get the horrible picture from just moments ago out of her mind.

Then came an electronic buzzing sound, and Winston's mom hurriedly took her phone from her pocket.

"Yes? Okay. Yes, I see."

Martha tried to read her face to guess if the cat was dead or alive, but she couldn't tell.

"No luck here," Winston's mom went on. "We've got to wait out this storm before we can even think about looking. We'll stay until you get back." There was a long pause, then, "Okay. I'll tell her."

Mrs. Cleary put the phone back in her pocket and said gently to Martha, "Your cat is badly hurt, but they're doing everything they can. They're not sure if she'll make it, but if she does, she's going to need surgery on her back legs. Your parents are going to be a while." She swallowed hard and said, "They asked the vet about how long the kittens could make it without their mom. The vet said it's hard to tell because we don't know the last time they were fed. But we need to find them within the next few hours."

"But we can't even start looking because of this stupid storm!" Martha screamed, then dissolved into tears again.

"Do you want to go lie down for a while?" Anand asked.

Martha shook her head through her sobs but let Sanjay and Winston drag her to her room, where she lay on her bed, still crying loudly.

Winston's mom came in and handed her a cup of water. "Sip this, sweetie," she said.

Martha took the cup just as a flash of lightning illuminated her bedroom. She closed her eyes. There was so much she didn't want to see.

"This is all my fault."

"What's all your fault, dear?"

Martha opened her eyes. They were all crowded around her with looks of concern. This made her feel even more guilty.

"It's my fault Mama Cat got hit. And it's my fault the kittens are going to starve to death! If the coyotes don't get them first." She paused to sob. When she got a little of her breath back she said, "I shouldn't have chased her down. I should have just let her be. She didn't need me. She was fine on her own and now...and now..."

Fresh sobs overtook her. Anne put a hand on her back. After a while, she got control of her breath and became aware that she was not the only one crying.

She looked up, horrified. "Anand!"

Anand was curled in a corner, sobbing as loudly as she had been and covered in tears and snot. Sanjay hovered over him with a helpless look on his face.

"Anand! I'm sorry!"

"I don't want the kittens to die! They can't die! We can't give up now! If it's your fault, then you have to fix it! You have to at least try!"

Martha stared at him. She'd never seen him cry like this before. She felt sick with herself. She wanted to crawl under her covers and fall asleep for a few months so this would all sort itself out on its own. But it was too late for that. She stood up from the bed and went to Anand, putting a hand on his shoulder as he crouched in the corner. "You're right, Anand. We've got to try. I can't promise we'll find them, but we're not giving up yet." Martha checked her watch. It was a quarter after seven.

"Hang on," said Winston's mom. "There's a thunderstorm out there. I can't let you run around the neighborhood when it's lightning out."

"It will be over soon. In the meantime, we can get ready," said Martha. She grabbed her notebook and opened it to a page full of numbers. "Can I use your phone?"

It was eight p.m. The lightning had stopped and the thunder could only be heard faintly in the distance. It was almost completely dark from all the storm clouds and the rain was still heavy, but Martha knew they couldn't wait any longer. Kittens could only live without their mom to feed them for maybe six hours. It had already been two hours since the car accident, and they had no way of knowing when the last feeding had been.

She led her troops, which now included Winston and his mom and all the neighbors who had answered their phones—Betty, Jim, and the lady two doors down—outside to the shed and started handing out flashlights and rain gear.

"We need to search between here and the park. Everybody fan out and track your route carefully so I know what's been checked. Grownups, you start at the park and work your way back this way. Boys, you start from here and don't head back until you meet up with Betty and Jim." Martha turned to Winston's mom. "Mrs. Cleary, I want to stay with you, in case you get another call."

Everyone nodded and set off in the rain, their flashlight beams cutting through the darkness and rain.

Martha and Winston's mom searched every yard along the path between her house and the house with the rickety fence. They saw at least a half dozen cats—yellow eyes glowing in the flashlight beams—lurking about and skittering off at their approach, but all were full grown. No kittens. In the yard behind Martha's house, a cat with long brown fur and a few patches of gold approached them and rubbed against her legs.

"You seen any kittens around?" Martha asked it. It made a small meow and stalked off again.

"Thanks for nothing," said Martha.

They searched for almost two hours. By the time they circled back to the house, the whole rest of the search party was slumped under the shelter by the side door. Her stomach dropped.

"Nothing?" Martha asked. Everyone shook their heads.

"Where'd you look?" She took her notebook from under her raincoat and began to document all the places her team had checked. They'd been very thorough. Every wheelbarrow, shed, and woodpile from here to the park had been searched. She checked her watch. It was nearly ten p.m. The kittens had been without their mother for at least five hours. The clock had run out.

She looked at Anand. His face was wet, but whether because of tears or rain, she couldn't tell. "I don't know what else to do, buddy. I think that's it. I think it's too late." Tears sprang to her eyes. "I'm so sorry. I tried"

Anand took a deep breath. "*We* tried. We didn't give up."

Martha hugged him, whispering as she did, "I just wish it had worked."

She turned back to her search party, holding back tears as she talked. "Thanks everybody. I really appreciate you coming out in the rain to try and help. Maybe in a few days we can all get together and have some kind of memorial service?" A few folks nodded.

"Martha, boys," said Winston's mom, "you should be

very proud of what you tried to do. You always had your heart in the right place. Sometimes these things just don't work out. Sometimes life doesn't go how you want it to."

Martha nodded. The tears came again.

"I guess you can all go home now," said Martha glumly. All her energy was gone, drained away like the rainwater into the gutter.

"We'll help you put all this stuff away," said Betty, pulling off her borrowed poncho. The rain had finally stopped altogether. The night was cool and damp. And so quiet.

"Thanks," said Martha, and she turned mechanically toward the backyard. At the door of the shed, the volunteers each handed over their gear, some offering words of sympathy and a hug. Jim was last. He put his hand on her shoulder and said, "If anyone could have found them, it would have been you, Martha. It just wasn't meant to be."

"Thanks, Jim," Martha sighed. "And thanks for helping us look."

"Goodnight," he said, waving his flashlight toward the coop. "And don't forget to check on your chickens. I see the door's still open."

"Oh right," said Martha distractedly. As Jim headed for home, she walked in the dark toward the coop, Anand and Sanjay falling into step with her.

"You're quiet," Martha said to Sanjay.

"I just don't know what to say. I know I said all along that we weren't going to find them, but...I can't believe we didn't find them."

"Maybe they were already, you know, dead?" Martha said.

"You mean, like maybe she abandoned all of them when she abandoned Willow?" Sanjay asked.

"Maybe. Who knows? All I know is they all would have been better off without me. And instead of Forty-two Days of Fun, we've had Forty-two Days of Cat." She slammed the coop door shut in frustration.

A high-pitched "mew!" came from inside the coop.

Martha froze.

"Did you guys just hear that?"

"Hear what?" Sanjay asked.

"Shhh!"

Then she heard it again, a tiny, high-pitched "meow!" as if a grown-up cat had been sucking in helium from a balloon. Every nerve in Martha's body went on alert. She'd stowed all the flashlights back in the shed. But Anand was still wearing his headlamp.

"Anand, turn that on, please," she said, pointing at his forehead.

Anand flicked the switch and Martha opened the door of the coop. They tiptoed inside with Anand in the lead. He shined his light all around. The chickens were sleep on the roosting bar, all nestled up against one another. Martha heard another mew and followed the sound. She grabbed Anand's head and pointed it at the nesting box.

A mass of furry little kittens—full of life—writhed in the beam of light.

19

UNFINISHED BUSINESS

The next morning, despite getting to bed so late, Anand woke up early with one thing on his mind. He stood on the rail of the bottom bunk, grabbed Sanjay's leg, and gave it a shake.

"Sanjay, wake up! Kittens!"

Sanjay grunted. Then raised his head and nodded. They hurried down two sets of stairs to the basement. Martha was already there. She smiled when she saw them. She was clutching a fluffy orange kitten. The boys joined her on the cool basement floor and Martha carefully placed the kitten in his lap. Anand held his good hand over its back, so it couldn't scurry away.

He couldn't believe the softness of the tiny cat's fur, or the sharpness of its claws.

"We should probably let them get used to us slowly," said Sanjay. Anand and Martha both sighed and put them back in the laundry basket. Anand wanted to clutch that cat to his chest forever.

"Okay," said Martha. "Kitty rest time. Let's go upstairs and think up some names."

Since there were four cats and four people who hadn't named a cat yet, Martha said everyone else should get to name one kitten.

"I'm naming one Schrödinger," said Uncle Marshall.

"I'll name one Olivia," said Martha's mom.

"That's my mom's name!" said Anand.

"And my favorite sister," said Auntie Fran.

Anand smiled.

"What are you naming that orange one who loves you so much, Anand?" Martha asked.

Anand paused for a moment. "I'm naming him Tarzan," he said and braced for Sanjay's teasing. But Sanjay only nodded.

Martha gave him a big smile.

"How about you, Sanjay?"

"I can't think of any good names," he said.

"Oh, come on," said Martha.

"You name it for me, Anand," Sanjay said. He seemed upset about something, but Anand couldn't tell what. Maybe he was still tired?

"Raptor!" said Anand without hesitation.

"Aw, that's cute," said Martha. "We've got Schrödinger, Olivia, Tarzan and Raptor." She was already writing the names down in her notebook.

"Now you just need to find homes for them," Auntie Fran said.

"But, Mom!" said Martha.

"Don't you remember our deal?"

Anand was a little surprised that deal would still stand given everything that had happened.

Martha eyes filled with tears. "What about Willow?"

"Now, Martha," said Auntie Fran sternly.

Anand sighed, thinking they were in for another family fight. But just then Auntie Fran's phone rang.

"Hello?"

Anand could tell by her face that this was news about Mama Cat. He moved a step closer to Martha. She was already upset. There was no telling what might happen if it was bad news. He might need to catch her if she fainted or something.

"Yes. Yes, I see." She paused and listened for a minute. Then she took a deep breath and said, "Well, if that's what you recommend, that's what we'll do. But I think you should know that we're only fostering this cat. It's a long story. We'll pay for the surgery, but would you be able to help us find a permanent home after she recovers?"

After she recovers! That must mean she was going to be okay. Martha was whispering, "Mom!"

Auntie Fran shook her head fiercely at Martha.

"Okay," Auntie Fran said into the phone. "Thank you all so much. Please keep me posted." She hung up.

"What's happening?" Martha asked.

"Mama Cat is stabilized, but they are going to have to do surgery." She paused.

"Why? For what?"

Auntie Fran swallowed and looked at each of them.

"To remove one of her back legs."

Anand gasped.

"The vet says cats do fine on three legs. She's pretty

confident everything will go well with the surgery and Mama Cat will be fine."

The kids were quiet as they took in this news. Finally, Martha said excitedly, "She'll be a tripod!"

"A tripod?" Anand asked, confused.

"Three legs, Anand," said Sanjay. "Like a camera stand."

"Oh right."

After breakfast, Anand lay in the fort, staring dolefully at his cast. Sanjay was next to him reading. With no chance of swinging on the Tarzan rope, he planned to pout his way through the rest of the trip. When he wasn't helping take care of the kittens, that is. It was hard to pout while holding a kitten.

"I'm going to do the chicken chores," he said, and shuffled outside.

He had just filled two water buckets and had one of them hooked over his left forearm when Sanjay joined him.

"You seem to be doing okay with just one arm," he said.

"No thanks to you," said Anand.

"Hey, I'm kinda sorry about that. I didn't think anything like that would happen."

Anand bit his lips together and gave his brother a serious look. "One arm isn't going to help me with the Tarzan rope. All I wanted to do was shut Winston up."

"He's not that bad. He helped find Mama Cat. Anyway, don't make him the reason," said Sanjay.

"It doesn't matter. Now it's not going to happen at all," said Anand and kicked over a water bucket.

Sanjay roughly took him by the cast. "Come with me."

They went to the shed, where Sanjay got a length of thick rope, and then walked back to the pear tree. Sanjay threw the rope up into the tree and tied the two ends together at about shoulder level.

"What if you could try swinging here and see if you've got enough strength in your left arm? I think you might."

Anand hesitated for a moment, remembering the pain of breaking his arm and not wanting a repeat with his other arm. "But here I'm not landing in water, I'm landing on the ground," said Anand.

"If you bend your knees, you'll be fine for the landing. You're planning for it; it's not the chickens knocking something out from under you. And besides, one thing I've noticed about you, you fall a lot, but you always get back up again."

It was, maybe, the nicest thing Sanjay had ever said to him.

Anand looked at the rope. He nodded, more to himself than to Sanjay. Then he dragged the step ladder over and climbed up on it.

He cradled his broken arm close to this body. Sanjay handed him the rope. He put it tightly under his left arm and took a deep breath.

He leaped off the chair and swung to the other side of the chicken yard. At the farthest arc of the swing, he jumped and bent his knees for landing. It was totally controlled. He had plenty of strength. He stood up straight and turned around, grinning.

"You got it," said Sanjay. "Told you so."

That afternoon they all headed off to the pool. Even Uncle Marshall came along. Of course, Winston was there. But Anand found he wasn't worried about him anymore. He was more worried about Martha knocking him down before he could get to the rope. She was jumping around like crazy, even more excited than he was.

"Good thing you got the waterproof cast!" she squealed.

He made a beeline toward the Tarzan rope. Winston, Martha, Sanjay, and Uncle Marshall followed. It was a long line.

"Uh, you're not actually going to do the rope swing with a broken arm are you? Are you right-handed?" Winston asked.

"Yes, I am right-handed. And watch me." Anand took his place in line.

"You're crazy," said Winston. "You're going to drown." Was that concern in his voice? Anand chose to keep ignoring him.

A few more kids to go and it would be his turn. He took some slow deep breaths.

Now he was up. The lifeguard eyed at him skeptically. "Are you sure?"

Anand nodded.

The lifeguard raised his sunglasses and exchanged

looks with another lifeguard at the next station over who shrugged, then pointed to Uncle Marshall and then the water.

"Sir," the lifeguard said to Uncle Marshall, "how about you get in the water to help him if he needs it."

Uncle Marshall hopped in the pool. Anand shook his head at him, trying to let him know that he didn't need any help.

"Just ignore me, Anand. You've got this," said Uncle Marshall.

Anand stepped onto the platform. He planted his feet firmly, about hip-width apart, and bent his knees slightly. He stared into the pool, but now it seemed to him to be a river cutting through the jungle. Piranhas were jumping out of the water, hungry for blood. The lifeguard handed him the rope. Before he could let himself think, he leaped off the pool deck and sailed over the water. Now! He released the rope, tucked up his knees, and hit the water in a perfect cannonball.

When he came up for air, he thrashed his good arm to knock out the piranhas and then dog-paddled the short distance to the side of the pool, right past his uncle. Martha was bouncing up and down on the pool deck, whooping for joy. Aunt Fran was cheering. And when he crawled out of the pool, Sanjay gave him a solid high five. Panting and full of pride, Anand walked proudly past Winston and got right back in line.

Many Tarzan swings later, Winston stopped Anand in the locker room. "Hey, it's pretty cool that you're not letting a broken arm stop you."

"Thanks," Anand muttered

"And I'm sorry I was, well, I'm sorry for the way I acted before. Are you coming to the pool next week?"

"No, we're going home to Minnesota on Sunday," said Anand.

"Oh, too bad, I wish we would have had more chances to hang out."

"Me too?" Anand wasn't quite so sure. "Well, gotta go."

"Ok, maybe see you next summer!"

"Um, yeah," said Anand.

As they were getting in the car, Winston came running out with a towel wrapped around him and yelling, "Hang on!"

They all turned to him.

"What about my kitten?"

"You'll have to come over and choose one," said Martha. "Have your dad call my mom."

"Okay, see you soon," said Winston.

Anand climbed in the car.

"See?" said Sanjay. "I told you he wasn't so bad."

20

THE DONATION

Mama Cat came home from the animal hospital with strict orders that she stay an indoor cat. She was still a skittish thing, that was for sure, and it wasn't just because she was now missing her left hind leg. When Martha brought her inside and let her out of the cat carrier, she streaked under Martha's bed and hadn't come out since.

"Poor little sweetheart," Martha fretted. They were all sitting on the floor in the hallway outside Martha's room so Mama Cat could have the room to herself. They kittens were crawling all over them.

"Sweetheart? Poor cat, yes. But I don't know how you're coming up with sweetheart. Only you could fall in love with a cat who clearly hates you," said Sanjay.

"She has every right to hate me," said Martha quietly. The poor thing hadn't had the chance to adjust and feel at home at Martha's house, she'd just given birth, then been hit by a car, had a stay at the animal hospital, lost a *leg*, and now was back where all the horror started for her.

"I've been thinking."

"Here comes the notebook," teased Anand.

"No, really. I don't think it's best for Mama Cat to be my cat. She needs to feel comfortable. *At home.* And she's not going to feel like that here." She looked up at the ceiling to try and keep the tears from coming.

"But where would she live then? Back where you got her?" Anand asked.

"Definitely not. But I don't know. That's the part I'm still thinking about."

They were quiet for a bit, watching Tarzan and Willow swat playfully at each other with their tiny paws.

"I have an idea, Martha," said Sanjay. "But I don't think you're going to like it."

"What is it?" she asked.

"You need to ask that cat guy, Jacob, what to do."

Martha stared at him, then looked for something to throw at him that wasn't a kitten. But then she sighed.

"Ugh. I think you're right."

Martha sat in the back seat of the car, clutching the money they had raised from the lemonade stand. Hopefully it would work as a peace offering to Jacob.

"Six dollars is better than nothing, right?" Martha asked.

"Barely," said Sanjay. She looked to Anand for agreement, but found that he was crying.

"Huh? What's the matter now?" Sanjay asked.

"Nothing. Leave me alone," Anand yelled.

"No, really," Martha said with concern. "What's wrong?"

He looked up at her. His face was red and streaked with tears.

"I just feel so bad for all those cats. Six dollars isn't going to do *anything*. We should have done more."

"You did the best you could," Martha's mom reassured him. Anand started crying even harder.

Everyone in the car got quiet. Martha's mom stopped at a red light. Martha saw her look of concern in the rearview mirror.

"He's right," said Sanjay. His voice was absolutely fierce.

Martha looked at him. His eyes were open wide, and he was staring straight out the front windshield like a zombie and crazily scratching his right hand.

"Catching one cat and finding two foster families is nothing." Sanjay growled. "The problem is huge."

The light turned green and her mom drove on.

"Stop!" shouted Sanjay.

Her mom flinched and glared at Sanjay in the rearview mirror. She kept on driving. "You guys have *got* to stop yelling 'stop' while I drive. What's wrong?"

"We have to turn around. I'm sorry. We've got to go back. I forgot something important. I'll explain when we get back to the house." Now Sanjay was crying. "Please turn around, Auntie Fran!"

What on earth was going on?

Martha's mom sighed and turned back in the direction of the house.

"Sorry," Sanjay said. "I'm sorry." He wiped tears on his T-shirt sleeve until it was soaked through.

At least Sanjay's crying had curbed Anand's meltdown. He was staring wide-eyed at his brother.

"Sanjay, what's going on?" asked Martha. "What did you forget?"

"I'll show you when we get back" was all she could get out of him.

When the car pulled into the driveway, Sanjay said, "Wait here," and dashed into the house and up the stairs to the crawl space. He counted back six rafters and slid his hand between the boards and insulation, retrieving the envelope of spending money.

Back at the car, he fanned out the money, revealing all three hundred dollars.

Martha gasped. "Where'd you get that?"

Sanjay swallowed. "It's the spending money my mom and dad gave us for the trip. I hid it because I wanted to keep it for myself to buy a bike."

"What?" yelled Anand.

Sanjay plowed on. "But I want the Cat People to have it, because they need all the help they can get. And I need to ask Anand, because it was supposed to be his money, too." His eyes were filling with tears again.

"Where did you hide it?" Anand asked.

"In the crawl space upstairs," said Sanjay.

"Good spot," said Martha.

"Anand, you can hit me if you want to. I deserve it."

Martha didn't let Anand answer that. "Oh, Sanjay," she said. "How wonderful! Anand, is it okay with you if the money goes to the Cat People?"

Anand muttered, "Way better the Cat People than him," then slugged him on the arm. He was definitely getting stronger. Sanjay rubbed the spot.

"And is it okay with you, Martha?" he asked. "I feel bad for making you pay for stuff. I'm sorry I lied about not having any spending money."

"Of course it's okay," said Martha. "Don't be silly."

"And I'm sorry I lied to you, Auntie Fran," he said. He couldn't confess fast enough. With each admission, he could feel all the anxiety of the past weeks finally leaking out of him. "You shouldn't have had to pay for us all summer, like at the amusement park and stuff."

Aunt Fran gave him the same patient smile his mother often did. "You're forgiven, dear boy," she said.

Sanjay sank back into his seat, feeling happier than he had the entire trip.

At the Cat People headquarters, Jacob was slouched behind the front desk. He didn't look thrilled to see them again. They told him the whole story about the Mama Cat getting hit, about finding the kittens and about their sad attempt at a lemonade stand. Then Martha told him how Sanjay and Anand were giving up all their summer spending money.

"Oh wow." His tone was still a little flat, but he actually smiled. "Three hundred and six dollars will buy about two hundred pounds of cat food, or pay for six neuterings, or buy medicine for sick cats."

"But we still have to find homes for four of the kittens," said Sanjay. "And we're leaving in a few days."

"I'm going to go bug my neighbor Betty again," said Martha. "She totally needs a kitten. Or four."

"Everyone needs at least four cats," Jacob said seriously.

"But there's one thing we really need your help with," said Martha, her tone changing from excited to serious. "Mama Cat can't stay with me. For one thing, my mom made me promise we'd only foster her, which I think I could have worked around." She shot a smirk at her mom. "But, the thing is, Mama Cat really hates me. I don't think she'd be happy at my house. We need to find a good place for her. Where she'll be happy."

"Or at least less *un*happy," Sanjay added. Martha was still being overly ambitious.

"And I don't want to just let her be an outdoor cat, off on her own," said Martha. "I'd worry too much that she'd get hit by a car again. Or other cats would be mean to her because she's different now."

"I see," said Jacob. "Tell me a little bit about her personality. That might help me find the right fit."

"She has three legs," Anand offered.

"That's not a personality trait, Anand," teased Sanjay.

"She likes things to be quiet," said Martha. "She doesn't like to be held."

"She doesn't like to be told what to do," said Anand.

"She wants to be free. Freeish," said Sanjay.

"Okay," said Jacob, looking thoughtful. "All that is

helpful. Let me make a few calls and see what I can come up with."

"Thanks, Jacob," said Martha. She even sounded sincere.

"Hey, can I get a picture of you guys? I'm going to write about your donation and put it in our next newsletter."

They posed in front of the big donation bin, Sanjay holding the wad of cash, all fanned out.

He was quiet on the way home. But this time it was a satisfied kind of quiet. His spirits got even higher when they saw Poppy and Bubbles—their little pygmy goat friends—in traffic. They were frolicking around in the back of the station wagon, probably on their way to the farm store.

21

DEPARTURES

I t was the last day of the visit. Martha and Sanjay slipped a note under Betty's screen door, rang the bell, and ran. They'd been doing this several times a day for the last three days in a final desperate attempt to get her to adopt a kitten. Winston's family was going to adopt one kitten, and then Winston had recruited one of his neighbors. That still left three cats who needed homes.

"Hey, stop!"

They froze midstride and turned around. Betty was leaning out of her door, shaking her head at them.

"You can stop leaving me notes now. I'll come and pick out a kitten this afternoon."

They ran back to her door. Martha gave her a big hug.

"I admire your perseverance, if not your methods," said Betty. "And Martha, you can be my pet sitter when I need one, as a consequence for getting me into this."

"I'd be happy to!" said Martha.

"Good. Because you'll be doing it for free," said Betty.

A few hours later, Martha was in her bedroom playing with Willow and the rest of the kittens, trying to pretend that it wasn't almost time to take Sanjay and Anand to the airport.

It had been a wonderful visit, better than she had even imagined. There'd been one last play session in the fort, one last ride on the tandem bike, one last load of laundry so the boys could greet their parents with fresh clothes. Yes, true, there had been puke and crying and a broken arm, but the fun they'd had! They had plowed through most of the Forty-Two Days of Fun List and had a bunch of great adventures she'd never imagined possible, like hiking through a rainforest and, of course, the kittens. Now they were packing up to go home.

Mama Cat would soon start the new life Jacob had found for her. She was going to become a rat patroller at a warehouse near the airport. She'd be indoors, and she wouldn't have to deal with people very much. She'd be freeish. Besides that, they'd succeeded in finding forever homes for three of the five kittens.

"Not only are the boys leaving me, but so are all of you," said Martha sadly to Schrödinger, Olivia, Tarzan, and Raptor as they lay curled in her lap, purring.

Winston had picked out his kitten that morning, choosing Raptor. He'd promised he'd keep the name and that Martha she could visit him anytime she wanted. And the boys, when they were visiting.

She didn't know how she was going to manage without the boys. They really did feel like brothers to her now.

Martha gave each kitten a squeeze. When she let them go, they started nibbling her toes. She shook them off. What could she do to distract herself until it was time to leave for the airport? She picked up a book but couldn't concentrate enough to read. She picked up some knitting. She'd gotten through one row when she heard a knock at her bedroom door.

"Come in," she said mournfully.

It was Sanjay and Anand.

"All done packing?" she asked.

"Yeah," said Sanjay. His expression was a mixture of gloom and anticipation. Martha understood because as sad as she was, she was happy that the boys would soon see their parents again. She couldn't imagine being away from her mom and dad for six weeks.

"Hey, how are you doing?" asked Anand.

A tear leaked from Martha's eye.

"Not good, huh?" said Sanjay. "Is it because you're grounded for a month the instant we leave?"

"What?" asked Martha. "Oh no. I totally forgot about that. That will be lame because Fern's coming back tomorrow."

Anand gave her a hug.

"Thanks, buddy. I guess we should look on the bright side," she said, trying to pull herself together. "We'll see each other again at Christmas. I made a countdown calendar in my notebook."

"Of course you did," said Sanjay.

"Look!" said Anand, pointing at his chest. "We put our wing pins back on."

"Oh! I'll put mine on, too," said Martha. "I'm going to

wear mine every day for the rest of the summer so I can remember this visit!"

Then they heard Martha's mom calling to them, and Martha's shoulders dropped. It was time to leave for the airport.

───────────

Her parents were in the dining room. They both had weird grins on their faces.

"Is it time to go?" said Martha.

"Almost," said her mom. "But we wanted to give you some good news while the boys are still here." Her mom and dad exchanged smiles.

"So, Martha," her father began. "Your mom and I have been thinking. We've noticed how devoted you've been to raising money for the Cat People and how well you've been taking care of the kittens. And we know that you want to keep Willow."

Martha held her breath.

"And we're going to let you," said her mom.

She jumped up and began bouncing all around the living room. She picked up Willow, clutched her above her face, and kissed her all over until the kitten started meowing in protest.

"Thank you!" she cried and gave her mom and dad a hug.

"Now then," said her mom, clearing her throat. "To business." She handed Sanjay some papers. "Your boarding passes, young man. Please inspect them for accuracy."

Martha read over Sanjay's shoulder as he leafed through them. PDX to MSP, Portland to Minneapolis. There was one with Sanjay's name and one with Anand's name. And there was a third paper that read, *Live animal boarding pass*.

Sanjay looked at his aunt with wide eyes.

She smiled at him. "That's Tarzan's ticket."

Martha squealed.

Martha's dad took that as his cue to pull a tiny cat carrier out from under the table.

"We talked to your parents. We told them how good you boys were with the cats, and how much you'd miss them, and how Tarzan still needed a family. They said you should bring him home with you," said Martha's mom.

Sanjay stood speechless. Anand ran off in search of Tarzan.

Martha was not just bouncing, but leaping. "This is perfect!" she cried. "Perfect, perfect, perfect!"

"I didn't even know this was possible!" said Sanjay. "I thought they were too little to go on a plane."

"They're too small for the cargo hold. He'll have to ride in the carrier under your seat," said Uncle Marshall.

Anand came back in with Tarzan.

"Okay," said Martha. "Sanjay, you've got to get some food and water ready for Tarzan to travel." She raised her finger to point at Anand and then stopped short. "Uh, how about you two figure it out, and I'll go put the bags in the car."

"Wow! Martha! You actually caught yourself!" said Sanjay. He gave her a high five.

"Better late than never," she mumbled, then grinned.

"But, Martha. Don't stop having good ideas and doing projects. You're pretty great at that stuff," said Sanjay.

When all the bags were loaded, Sanjay, Martha, and Anand let Tarzan say goodbye to all the other kittens. They simply tried to eat one another's heads, as they always did.

"It'd be nice to be a cat and not know when it was goodbye, so you wouldn't get so sad," said Martha.

Sanjay and Anand nodded.

On the ride to the airport, they recapped their visit and they agreed that of course their favorite event was discovering the kittens. Tarzan meowed in agreement.

Reality set in when they reached the parking ramp. No one said a word as Martha's dad unloaded their luggage from the trunk. It was a sad train of kids who dragged themselves through the big revolving doors.

Going through security took a long time because the boys had to get special wristbands to fly alone and Martha and her parents had to get a special pass so they could take the boys all the way to their plane. And the security people made a fuss over how cute Tarzan was.

When they were through, instead of going directly to the gate for the plane to Minneapolis, they stopped a few gates away, where there were no flights taking off.

"This is a quieter space to say goodbye," said Martha's mom, her voice catching in her throat.

Martha's parents gave the boys a long, tight hug.

"Thank you both so much for coming. We loved

having you; it was a great treat to spend so much time with our nephews," Martha's mom said.

Martha wiped away a tear and thrust out her chin. "I'm so happy for you guys—getting to go home to your parents and getting to keep Tarzan."

The kids hugged again and again. Martha didn't really have the right words to match her feelings.

A fuzzy voice announced that boarding was beginning for the Portland to Minneapolis flight. The boys gathered up their things and headed for the gate.

Martha watched them walk away. What a trip it had been! Forty-two days of fun that the three of them would never forget. And, Martha had to admit, better than anyone could have planned.

ABOUT THE AUTHOR

Sue Campbell is a word merchant. Both a writer and a book marketer, getting stories into the world is what she's all about. She cohosts The Mommy's Pen Podcast with her twelve-year-old daughter where they talk about and dissect stories.

Sue lives with her husband, two daughters, eight chickens, and a super messy rabbit on a quasi-urban farm in Portland, Oregon. And yes, Portland *is* that weird.

Subscribe to her newsletter and get special bonus content for both parents and kids:

suecampbellbooks.com/subscribe

ACKNOWLEDGMENTS

I am here to tell you, no one book is the work of a single person. I'd like to thank the following individuals for their help in creating this book: Anne Hawley, Xina Uhl, John Bray and Rachelle Ramirez: thanks for the feedback via our Super Hardcore Editing Group (SHEG).

Marinda Valenti, thanks for your excellent copyediting work. Maeve Norton, thank you for the book cover illustration and design of my dreams.

Thank you to Ayanna Coleman, my first agent, for believing in the book early on.

Thanks to my brother-in-law for input on Indian-American culture.

Thank you to the many beta readers, both grown-ups and kids, who read not-very-good drafts (in no particular order): Kristin Glasbergen, Bethany and Vivian Widick, Denise Ronek Welch and Ada, Audrey Morris, Amy Beacom, Luca and Maggie DiMezza, Jenna Beacom, Erica Fuson, Deborah Campbell, Kirsten Peters, Lee Ann

Moldovanyi, Tanya Zivkovic, Katie Popoff, and the fifth/sixth grade class at Ivy School from 2017/2018: Zella, Ruby, Ruby, Simon, Donovan, Isabel, Mia, Nora, Kalista, Wanette, Nate, Linden and Kadan.

It took me a long time to write this pretty slim book, so I really hope I haven't forgotten anyone. Finally, a huge thank you to my daughter Nora. Without you, this book would never have been written.